Lindsay Swift

The Massachusetts Election Sermons

An essay in descriptive bibliography. Vol. 1

Lindsay Swift

The Massachusetts Election Sermons
An essay in descriptive bibliography. Vol. 1

ISBN/EAN: 9783337114046

Printed in Europe, USA, Canada, Australia, Japan

Cover: Foto ©Raphael Reischuk / pixelio.de

More available books at **www.hansebooks.com**

THE

MASSACHUSETTS ELECTION SERMONS

An Essay

IN

DESCRIPTIVE BIBLIOGRAPHY

BY LINDSAY SWIFT

REPRINTED FROM

THE PUBLICATIONS

OF

The Colonial Society of Massachusetts

VOL. I.

CAMBRIDGE

JOHN WILSON AND SON

University Press

1897

NOTE.

Since this Essay was printed in the Transactions of The Colonial Society of Massachusetts, Mr. Abner C. Goodell, Jr., has informed me that the indictments against Philip English charge an offence committed after the date of Moody's sermon, and that Bentley's statements (p. 20, *post*) must be taken with plenty of salt. To the same competent authority I am indebted for the further information that John Rogers of Ipswich and the "Rev. Mr. Rogers of Boxford" were not the two persons whose pamphlets were ordered by the General Court to be burned (p. 29, *post*). The eccentric two John Rogerses — father and son — were from New London, Connecticut. (Province Laws, VIII., 155, 555.) Unhappily, I followed Sibley.

L. S.

Boston, 4 March, 1897.

On Wednesday, 7 January, 1885, the General Court of Massachusetts met to organize; the two branches of the Legislature chose their presiding and other officers, and then adjourned to the next day. In obedience to an Act passed, on 6 March, 1884, "To repeal the Public Statutes relating to the Annual Election Sermon,"[1] there was omitted from the ceremonies incident to the day an ancient custom, without the observance of which the legislators of earlier days would not have had the temerity to begin their public duties. For some years previously, the delivery of the sermon had been tacitly acknowledged to have been persevered in more through respect for honorable precedent than as a sincere expression of the religious and political spirit of the age; accordingly this last slight interdependence in the Commonwealth between Church and State had few to mourn its extinction, with the exception perhaps of some persistent admirers of the *tempus actum*.

In common with all that falls into disuse, the Election Sermon will soon survive only in the memory of a few, and therefore an attempt is here made to collect whatever may prove of popular or antiquarian interest concerning so venerable an observance. Listening to sermons is not infrequently dry work, and reading about sermons may be still drier; notwithstanding this, the present subject is so interwoven with the literature and the political concerns of Massachusetts during its entire history as Colony, Province, Colony, State, and Commonwealth, that it cannot be devoid of value, though the narrative may be arid indeed. Macaulay once said that nobody had ever read the whole of the "Faerie Queene;" since this statement many, through sheer persistency,

---

[1] Acts and Resolves, 1884, chap. 60.

have pushed through that meritorious but extended poem, as if it were a sort of feat which they had been dared to perform. Will any one take the assertion as a challenge, when I admit that I have read with more or less care every one of these sermons known to have been printed — more than two hundred in number? In all probability the Rev. John Pierce and the late Mr. John Wingate Thornton were conversant with the contents of most of these discourses. Both were collectors of Election Sermons, and to them, as well as to others who have taken an interest in this subject, due acknowledgment will be made.

What, then, was the Annual Election Sermon, so dear to the past, yet abolished in a fit of spleen, as it were, after two hundred and fifty years of observance?

Precisely how this custom originated will probably never be known. The Massachusetts Colony Records and Winthrop's Journal are all the sources of information which we have, or are likely to have, and the memoranda therein contained are scant. It is, however, certain that there was no sermon between 1628 and 1630, for the patent and government of the Plantation were not transferred to America until 1630, when the Records of the Governor and Company begin.[1] Although the Assistants and Deputies met for election, as by charter appointed, as early as 1630, there is no mention of any attendant religious ceremony until 1634. Thornton says: " The origin of this anniversary is to be found in the charter . . . which provided that ' one governor, one deputy-governor, and eighteen assistants, and all other officers of the said companie,' — not of the colony, — should be chosen in their ' general court, or assemblie,' on ' the last Wednesday in Easter Terme, yearely, for the yeare ensuing.' "[2]   On 14 May, 1634, the General Court assembled. John Winthrop had been chosen Governor up to this time, and it was now thought that possibly his re-election was in danger. John Cotton accordingly preached a political sermon, urging strongly that Winthrop should again be chosen. Whether his hearers did not relish a minister's interference with politics, or whether at that early day Cæsarism was felt to be a menace, Mr. Cotton's effort failed of its desired result, and Thomas Dudley was chosen Governor. Although this effort of Cotton's may be con-

---

[1] Massachusetts Colony Records, i. 73.
[2] Thornton's Pulpit of the American Revolution, p. xxiii.

sidered to have been a regular Election Sermon, it would appear that it was preached before the votes were thrown, whereas the sermon was usually delivered after the choice was made, and was addressed to the outgoing administration.

Cotton Mather, who calls Cotton a "walking library," says: "The good Spirit of God, by that Sermon, had a mighty Influence upon all Ranks of Men, in the Infant Plantation; who from this time carried on their Affairs, with a new Life, Satisfaction, and Unanimity."[1] Hutchinson speaks of the sermon (but by mistake putting it a year later) as one which "carried the point against the plebeians," that is, the Deputies, who were in favor of the removal of Hooker to Connecticut.[2]

Mr. Henry II. Edes, without the help of whose list of Election Sermons, published in 1871 in connection with Grinnell's sermon for that year, I should never have made my present attempt, is probably mistaken in giving the text of Cotton's May sermon as Haggai ii. 4. On 24 August of the same year, however, Cotton did preach from that text, to the evident gratification of Winthrop and the Court.[3]

I have described at some length the inauguration of the custom by Cotton; it was henceforth continued, as the Rev. Albert Barnes writes, in "a belief that religion and law were closely connected."[4] Inasmuch as the compilers of previous lists of the Election Sermons have not sought to describe the earlier discourses, but have furnished only the names of the preachers, their residences, the colleges at which they graduated, and the texts of their sermons, I shall make no apology for entering somewhat fully into the early history of this subject, especially since I am really breaking new ground, no effort having until now been made, in print, to discover what sermons were actually delivered and printed, and what delivered and not printed.

[1] Magnalia (edition of 1702), Book iii. p. 21. Mather may refer here to the sermon which Cotton preached on 24 August.

[2] History of Massachusetts Bay (edition of 1764), i. 45.

[3] Winthrop's Journal (edition of 1853), i. 168.

[4] See "Election Sermons," a disappointing article, by Barnes in the "Christian Spectator," vol. x. It is merely a review of some Connecticut and New Hampshire sermons, in which the reverend reviewer finds "an occasion for offering some considerations on the influence of religion and law."

If there were sermons in 1635 and 1636, we have no record of them. In 1637, Thomas Shepard, whom Captain Edward Johnson, in his "Wonder-working Providence," calls "that "gratious sweete Heavenly minded, and soule-ravishing Minister," [1] is known to have preached, but from what text has not been ascertained. The Rev. John Wheelwright had just been adjudged guilty of sedition for inveighing, at last Fast, "against all that walked in a covenant of works." [2] Preaching before the conflicting factions in this affair, Shepard, "at the day of election, brought them yet nearer, so as, except men of good understanding, and such as knew the bottom of the tenents of those of the other party, few could see where the difference was." [3]

We must infer that Shepard's preaching was both powerful and convincing from an incident which Winthrop mentions of one Turner of Charlestown who was so "wounded in conscience" at a sermon by Shepard that he "drowned himself in a little pit where was not above two feet water." [4] The next year, 1638, Shepard preached again, and this sermon is the first of which we have anything like a full text. By one of those happy discoveries which sometimes gladden the historian's heart, Mr. John Ward Dean was so fortunate as to fall upon a skeleton of this interesting discourse, in manuscript, which he published in October, 1870. [5] Both Mr. Dean and Mr. Edes give satisfactory accounts of it. It was preached a year after the defeat of Vane and his party, and the text "Then sayd all the trees to the Bramble raine ouer vs " [6] indicates plainly the line of thought. Shepard speaks of the "multitude" choosing a bad governor, and advises "Wᵐ brambles do appeare call for hatchets do not deale gently it will prick you." The conservatism of the clergy had begun to show itself in such a sermon as this, which attests the truth of what Samuel Stone ("Doctor irrefragabiles," Cotton Mather must add) said of the government of Congregationalism, that "it was a speaking Aristocracy in the Face of a silent Democracy." [7] This Democracy was, however, soon to become audible even in regard to these very Election Sermons.

[1] Johnson's Wonder-working Providence (Poole's edition, 1867). p. 77.
[2] Winthrop's Journal. i. 256.   [3] *Ibid.* i. 264.   [4] *Ibid.* ii. 73.
[5] New England Historical and Genealogical Register, xxiv. 361–366.
[6] Judges, ix. 14. 15.   [7] Magnalia, Book iii. p. 118.

To return a moment to Shepard's sermon. It is noteworthy that Ezra Stiles, in a letter to Hutchinson, writes, "I have also a copy of the Election Sermon preached by the minister of Cambridge, I think, Mr. Shepard, when Mr. Vane was dropped." [1] Mr. J. Hammond Trumbull is of the opinion that the manuscript from which President Stiles's copy was extracted was probably written out from the short-hand notes of some hearer. Mr. Dean believes it possible that the sermon may have been preached the day after the Court met.

The preachers for 1639 and 1640 are not known.

Although the Magistrates and the Deputies still sat together, and continued to do so until 1644, there are already evidences of misunderstandings. An increasing friction is plainly discoverable in Winthrop's ample account of Nathaniel Ward's sermon for 1641.[2] Ward was the famous Simple Cobbler of Agawam who drew up the "Body of Liberties," [3] and espoused the popular side as his sermon plainly shows.

Barry draws largely upon Winthrop regarding Ward's sermon in 1641, and Rogers's in 1643, to show that the colonists were by this time "a race of politicians." "As in the army of Xenophon, so in Massachusetts, boundless liberty of speech was indulged; and the magistrates and the clergy . . . were as earnest as any." [4]

No sermon is known to have been preached in 1642; perhaps the town of Boston was in too excitable a condition to listen, for its public temper had now waxed warm over the famous 'Sow business,' — a mighty matter in its day. The supposed unlawful seizure of a stray sow, by Captain Robert Keayne, later the town's benefactor, from the keeping of a poor woman, served to widen the division between plebeians and patricians. We may fairly infer, then, that in his Election Sermon for 1643, Ezekiel Rogers of Rowley was fostering that "democratical spirit which acts our deputies," [5] when he earnestly sought to dissuade them from reelecting the good Winthrop.

---

[1] New England Historical and Genealogical Register, xxvi. 162.

[2] Winthrop's Journal, ii. 42; quoted also in Lechford's Plain Dealing (Trumbull's edition), p. 68.

[3] Printed in 3 Massachusetts Historical Collections, viii. 191.

[4] History of Massachusetts, i. 329–332.

[5] Winthrop's Journal, ii. 111.

Cotton Mather may have had Rogers's sermon in mind when he said that "Sermons were Preached at the Anniversary Court of Election, to disswade the Freemen from chusing One Man Twice together."[1]

Although Rogers's appeal was unsuccessful (for Winthrop was again elected), yet he had shown that he stood for the claimant of the sow, one Sherman's wife, as against Captain Keayne, who was "accounted a rich man, and she a poor woman." This all may seem trivial now, but it was not so in fact, and the sermon was important on this account alone; at least Cotton Mather seemed to think so, when he wrote, " though the Occasion and the Auditory were *Great*, yet he shew'd his Abilities to be *Greater;* insomuch, that he became famous through the whole Country."[2]

In the " Massachusetts Colony Records " is an interesting entry relating to the year 1643–4: " Mr Madder to bee desired to p̄pare himselfe to p̄ach to ye assembly at ye next Co^{r}t of Election."[3] A little further is a still more interesting minute : " It is ordered, the printer shall have leave to print the election sermon, wth Mr Mathers consent, & the artillery sermon, wth Mr Nortons consent."[4]

This "Mr. Madder" was of course, Richard, grandfather of Cotton Mather, who calls him one of the "angelical men," or, anagrammatically, "a third charmer." Curiously enough, the pedantic grandson praises Richard Mather for a chariness of " Citation of Latine Sentences." Cotton Mather, in his sermon on Higginson in 1709, calls John Higginson's sermon for 1663 the " *First-Born* by the way of the Press, of all the *Election Sermons* that we have in our Libraries ; " thus showing that he did not know that Richard Mather's sermon was printed, if indeed it ever was. [5]

Permission by the Court to print was not a simple act of courtesy, for it is well understood that there was a censorship of the press ; even as late as 1669 the printing of Thomas à Kempis's " De Imitatione " was inhibited, that work being written by a " Popish minister ; "[6] and I have noted that Shepard's sermon in 1672 bears the *imprimatur* of Urian Oakes and John Sherman.

[1] Magnalia, Book ii. p. 10.   [2] *Ibid.* Book iii. p. 102.
[3] Massachusetts Colony Records, ii. 62.   [4] *Ibid.* ii. 71.
[5] See note by Dr. George H. Moore in Historical Magazine, February, 1867, p. 116.
[6] Massachusetts Colony Records, iv. Part ii. p. 424.

Furthermore the expense of printing was probably not borne by the public. This was the opinion of the late Dr. George H. Moore,[1] who seemed to know of evidence extant "that the painful preacher had to depend upon the liberality of some of the pious ' persons of worth' for the preservation of his sermons in type." Printed or not, Mather's sermon is in all probability lost to us.

The old trouble between the Magistrates and Deputies broke out again, and more violently, in 1645. Barry says, "The most exciting discussions, however, were between the Magistrates and the Deputies. One of these related to the appointment of the court preachers. At first, such appointments were made by the Assistants; but when the House of Deputies was established, they claimed the appointing power."[2] The importance attached by contemporaries to a matter apparently so simple as the choice of an election preacher, is shown by the space given by Winthrop in his Journal to the dispute between the Deputies, who had chosen Mr. Norton, and the Magistrates and Governor, who had chosen Mr. Norris of Salem.[3]

Mr. Norton, the choice of the popular body, did preach, no doubt to the sorrow of men like Winthrop, who may at this juncture have felt with Richard Saltonstall that such things were a "sinful innovation." The result of all this trouble was that, beginning with the year 1646, the preachers were chosen on alternate years by the Magistrates and Deputies. It appears that Edward Norris of Salem, the choice of the magistrates under the new arrangement, preached, and that the Court was "carried on with much peace and good correspondency; and when the business was near ended, the magistrates and deputies met, and concluded what remained, and so departed in much love."[4] There is no reason to doubt Winthrop's accuracy, but it is worth noting that, according to the Colony Records, Nathaniel Rogers was chosen by the Deputies.[5] I am inclined to think, and I believe it was the opinion of Dr.

[1] Manuscript note now in Boston Public Library.
[2] History of Massachusetts, i. 331.
[3] Winthrop's Journal, ii. 268.   [4] *Ibid.* ii. 316.
[5] Itt being the time & turne of y⁰ Depu for to choose & appointe y⁰ ministe to p'each the se'mon at y⁰ next Cou'te of Elecčon, they chose & desired M Nathaniell Roge's, of Ipswich, to p'each y⁰ next elecčon sermon. (Massachusetts Colony Records, iii. 80.)

Moore, that Rogers should be assigned to the year 1647; if this supposition is correct, a blank in Mr. Edes's list is filled. My reason is, of course, that the Magistrates having, without question, had their choice in 1646, the next year's choice belonged by right to the Deputies.

In 1648, Zechariah Symmes of Charlestown preached, and although we have not his sermon, the loss is not, in this busy age, much to be deplored, for Captain Johnson says that this remarkable man on one occasion "continued in preaching and prayer about the space of four or five houres."[1] His fecundity was not confined to the pulpit, for he was the father of thirteen children. To quote Johnson again, he was a "reverend and painfull minister," and according to Mather, "a *Sufferer* for what he preach'd."[2] Nor has the sermon of Thomas Cobbett, who preached in 1649, survived. Cobbett was, however, requested to print. "Itt was voted, that Mr Speaker, in the name of the Howse of Deputyes, should render Mr Cobbett the thankes of the howse for his worthy paines in his sermon, w^{ch}, at the desire of this howse, he preached on the day of elecͤon, & declare to him it is their desire he would print it heere or elsuhere."[3]

Between the years 1650 and 1655, inclusive, there is a lamentable gap. During these and earlier years, it is probable that sermons were delivered, and we may suppose that prominent men were chosen to preach. During the last years of the observance of this custom, ministers not always of the first importance were honored by an invitation to preach, but in the early days no inferior names are found upon the list. Jonathan Mitchel may have preached at this period. Of him I shall speak presently.

In 1656, "M^r. Charles Chauncey, præsident of Harvard Colledg, is desired to preach before the Gennerall Court on the next election day."[4] His sermon was not, I think, one of his "printed composures."

Although he had been the "people's choice" in 1645, John Norton again preached in 1657,[5] and for the third time in 1661.

---

[1] Johnson's Wonder-working Providence. p. 178.

[2] Magnalia, Book ii. p. 131.

[3] Massachusetts Colony Records, iii. 148.   [4] *Ibid.* iv. Part i. 254.

[5] In a copy of Oakes's sermon for 1673, which belonged to Samuel Sewall, is a manuscript memorandum, which, Sewall says, was "taken out of Grand-

It is a misfortune that Jonathan Mitchel's sermon for 1658 does not exist, for we are assured in the "Magnalia" that his utterance has a "becoming tunableness and vivacity," although his sermons "smelt of the lamp." Mather further speaks of his preaching "as a very lovely song of one that hath a pleasant Voice;" but, unhappily, we learn later that he "soon grew extream Fat."[1] Sibley, in his "Biographical Sketches of Graduates of Harvard University," does not mention this sermon of 1658. As a political orator, Mitchel must be judged by his later sermon of 1667. There is a possibility that he may have preached before 1657, for Mather says "His *Great Worth* caused him to be called forth several times with an *Early* and *Special* Respect from the *General Court* of the Colony, to preach on the Greatest Solemnity that the Colony afforded; Namely, *The Anniversary Election of Governour and Magistrates*."[2] Potent, indeed, must have been his exhorting, if the lines of F[rancis?] Drake[3] are to be taken seriously: —

"The *Quaker* trembling at his *Thunder* fled;
And with *Caligula* resum'd his Bed."[4]

John Eliot preached in 1659; this fact alone is all that seems to be known of his sermon. In 1660 Richard Mather again preached; and although there is no direct evidence that the sermon was printed, yet in Mitchel's sermon for 1667 is an allusion to it, in which the text and a part of the substance are quoted, as follows: —

"So of old in the Wilderness, *Psal.* 77. 20. Which Text of Scripture we heard well improved in a Sermon on the like occasion now Seven years ago; wherein it was said, That that was the Thirtieth year currant that God had given us godly *Magistrates*: if so, this is the Thirty seventh year currant, wherein we have enjoyed that mercy. Whereupon

father Hull's Character Book of several that did preach the Artillery and Election sermons," in which Mr. Flint is set down as preacher in 1657, and Mr. Ward as preacher in 1660. Neither of these names seems to be correct, yet this memorandum as a whole, no doubt, has been important in determining some of the preachers. It is in the Prince collection, now in the Boston Public Library.

[1] Magnalia, Book iv. 184.　　　[2] *Ibid.* Book iv. 182.
[3] I have been unable to identify this "F. Drake," and only offer the bracketed name as a suggestion.
[4] Magnalia, Book iv. 185.

it was then solemnly added (by that Reverend Servant of God who then Preached) That the Sun shines not upon an happier people than we are in regard of this mercy." [1]

This close following of Mather's words is itself good reason for supposing that Mitchel either saw a printed or a manuscript copy, or else that he possessed an excellent memory or a well-kept diary. With the year 1660 end the dark ages of the Election Sermon. During twenty-seven years, 1634–1660 inclusive, fifteen sermons are known to have been preached by twelve different persons, and of these fifteen not one is known to have been printed, although the Cambridge press had been running since 1640. Two of the preachers, we are sure, were asked to print; but as this seems only to imply that the printing was as yet a private venture, it is probable that it was not undertaken in either case.

John Norton's " Sion the Out-cast healed of her Wounds," preached in 1661, and printed in his " Three Choice and Profitable sermons " (Cambridge, 1664), was, it is usual to say, the first Election Sermon which was printed. While it was first in the chronological series of sermons to be printed, it was not actually the first to be sent to the press. That distinction belongs to John Higginson's for 1663, which appeared the same year in which it was delivered. Norton's effort is one of the most eccentric of the many curious productions in this long series. He himself calls it "a Divine Plaister for a Sin-sick Out-cast;" [2] and, carrying out his pathological metaphor, he says, " God will apply a sanative Cataplasm, an healing Plaster." [3] As in the case of the probably accidental " dissemble or cloak," or the " acknowledge and confess " of the Book of Common Prayer, he here uses pedantic Latin and common English in parallelisms. His tropes were often pushed to the extreme limits of good taste, as when he says " that Davids tears fall into Gods bottle, is matter of joy." [4] A merit of the sermon, not common to most of its kind in this era, is its brevity.

Nothing is known of the sermon for 1662.

" The Cause of God and his People in New-England," by Higginson, also a meritoriously brief performance, was delivered and

¹ Mitchel's " Nehemiah on the Wall," p. 23.
² Norton's " Sion the Out-cast," p. 1.   ³ Ibid. p. 2.   ⁴ Ibid. p. 6.

printed in 1663, and is, beyond doubt, what Cotton Mather, in 1709, said it was, "the *first born*, by way of the press, of all the *Election Sermons*, that we have in our libraries." It is, as a matter of course, strong in favor of Non-toleration; nor does its author fail to remind his hearers "that *New-England is originally a plantation of Religion, not a plantation of Trade*. Let Merchants and such as are increasing *Cent per Cent* remember this."[1] This sentence shows him to have been the vigorous preacher to whose virtues Nicholas Noyes, in his Elegy, bears testimony: —

> " Young to the Pulpit he did get,
> And Seventy Two Years in 't did sweat."[2]

For the third and last time Richard Mather, in 1664, preached before the Court of Elections; he could have had none of the fondness for appearing in print on the least pretext, so prominent in his son Increase and grandson Cotton, for he seems again to have failed to commit his sermon to the press.

The sermons of John Russell for 1665, and of Thomas Cobbett for 1666, were not printed, so far as can be discovered. Russell was, I believe, then quietly preaching at Hadley, but it may be that his sermon came under the ban of a rigid sectarian censorship. Sibley says of Russell, "in 1665 he preached the Massachusetts Election Sermon from Psalm cxii. 6[3]: probably not published."[4] In Russell's house at Hadley, Whalley and Goffe lived for some years.

The text of Cobbett's sermon is referred to in Mitchel's sermon for the next year as 2 Chronicles xv. 2.

Jonathan Mitchel's sermon for 1667[5] was not printed until 1671, after his death. It is one of the great sermons of those days, and is particularly "sound" against anabaptism, toleration, and Separatists. Increase Mather quotes from it approvingly in the preface to Torrey's discourse of 1674.

[1] Higginson's "The Cause of God . . .", p. 11.
[2] New-England Historical and Genealogical Register, vii. 239.
[3] Edes says from Psalm cxxii. 6.   [4] Sibley's "Graduates," i. 117.
[5] The title is curious enough to give entire: "Nehemiah on the Wall in Troublesom Times; or, a Serious and Seasonable Improvement of that great Example of Magistratical Piety and Prudence, Self-denial and Tenderness, Fearlessness and Fidelity, unto Instruction and Encouragement of present and succeeding Rulers in our Israel."

At the election of 1668, a famous discourse was preached by William Stoughton, which was so well liked that the Governor himself presented to the preacher the thanks of the General Court, and a request to prepare it for the press.[1]   It was printed in 1670. The printing was done at private expense, for in the Advertisement a "Person of Worth" is spoken of, who adventures "the publishing, of what the pious Author was well-nigh invincibly unwilling should ever have come forth."[2]   It is strong intellectually, and contains many fine passages; one, in particular, impressed me, in which are rehearsed the sins of New England.[3] There appear to have been, to the *sæva indignatio* of Stoughton, few sins of which New England was then innocent, and the violence of his wrath bears out the statement in his epitaph that Stoughton was "Impietatis & Vitij Hostis Acerrimus."

There were two editions of Stoughton's sermon : the first edition has thirty-eight pages; and the second forty pages, of which the last two pages were in finer type.   For the second edition the type was probably reset, though both were issued in the same year.   An abridgment occupies a few pages of " Elijah's Mantle " (Boston, 1722; 1774), and selections are reprinted as appendixes to Prince's Election Sermon for 1730.

In this sermon occurs the famous saying of Stoughton, "God sifted a whole Nation that he might send choice Grain over into this Wilderness."   Longfellow no doubt had this in mind in the "Courtship of Miles Standish" when he says, "God had sifted three kingdoms to find wheat for this planting."

It is generally supposed that the sermon for 1669 by John Davenport — whom the Indians called "so big study man "— was never printed, but in the " Magnalia " I find the following : " Nor would I forget a Sermon of his on 2 Sam. 23, 3, at the Anniversary Court of Election at Boston, 1669, afterwards published."[4]

A good " doctrinal " sermon has always been a test of a preacher's ability in New England.   But it seems to me, as I have reviewed this long stretch of years, in which over seven generations of clergy and laymen have lived, that the spirit of religion has persistently grown better, at least more refined.   The early dis-

---

[1] Massachusetts Colony Records, iv. Part ii. 376.
[2] Stoughton's " New-England's True Interest," p. 3.   [3] *Ibid.* p. 20.
[4] Magnalia, Book iii. p. 56.

courses were full of ecclesiasticism, theology, and good politics, but of humanity, brotherly kindness, and what is now understood by Christianity, I have been able to discern very little. Nor is this hard to explain. The ministers then were important factors in society, and in many cases, by their great learning, and their social remoteness from their laity, inevitably had little in common with those among whom they most faithfully and earnestly labored.

In view of these facts, we can understand in what spirit Cotton Mather commends such a sermon as Samuel Danforth preached in 1670. To Mather, Danforth was eminent because he was "a notable *Text*-Man, and one who had more than Forty or Fifty *Scriptures* distinctly quoted in One Discourse." [1] The following metaphorical sentence from Danforth's sermon seems worth repeating: "Such as escape the *Lime-pit* of Pharisaical Hypocrisie, fall into the *Coal-pit* of Sadducean Atheism and Epicurism." [2]

The J. O. who preached in 1671 was John Oxenbridge, and his sermon is now exceedingly rare.

If it were possible or desirable to pick out the "best" from over two hundred sermons, I should be inclined to choose Thomas Shepard's famous "Eye-Salve" which he preached in 1672, and which is worth mentioning somewhat fully. There is no doubt that there is in it "*Constellated* . . . much Learning, Wisdom, Holiness and Faithfulness," [3] but it also is, as Mr. Thornton wrote in his own copy, "of much historical interest and value." So many of its sentences have passed into our literary inheritance that it may well be held as an American classic. With Stoughton, Shepard is opposed to all false liberalism, as when he says: "'T is Satan's policy, to plead for an indefinite and boundless toleration." [4] He is plainly paraphrasing Stoughton in an almost equally familiar sentence: "The Lord sowed this land at first with such precious seed-corn, as was pickt out of our whole Nation." [5] He calls Laud — at least Laud seems to be the person meant — a "Bear" [6] a "ravening wolf," and a "Fox." [7] The Quakers, always an object of animadversion in the Election Sermon, are the "brood of the

---

[1] Magnalia, Book iv. p. 154, § 5.
[2] Danforth's Election Sermon for 1670, p. 15.
[3] Magnalia, Book iv. p. 191, § 5.
[4] Shepard's "Eye-Salve," p. 14.
[5] *Ibid.* p. 12.
[6] *Ibid.* p. 13.
[7] *Ibid.* p. 13.

Serpent."[1]   I must not forget to add that Shepard pleads nobly to have " Foundations laid for *Free-Schools*, where poor Scholars might be there educated by some Publick Stock."[2]   The need of adequate schools, especially of "inferiour" schools, as they were called, was continually presented in these sermons, down to the middle of the last century.

A closely printed small quarto of seventy pages, comprises the sermon for 1673, by Urian Oakes, of whom it is said that he had been seen to turn his hour-glass four times during a service!   He is not behind Shepard in hating toleration as the "first born of all Abominations," though "heartily for all due Moderation."   It is clear that authors then had the same impressive modesty as now, for the address to the "Christian Reader" tells the old coy story that, by "the concurrent and importunate intreaties of very many his Brethren . . . he hath been at last prevailed with, to permit it to pass through the press."   Cotton Mather, in saying of Oakes, "America never had a greater master of the true, pure Ciceronian Latin language," shows his pleasure at the use of such words as "succenturiation"[3] and "recidivation."[4]   This Latinist could also use his mother tongue to good effect in hurling epithets at "wanton Gospellers," "giddy Professors," "petty Politicians," and "little creeping Statesmen" who busied themselves in "lying and calumniating men of piety worth and authority."   His sermon was important, besides having, I believe, the longest title to be found in the whole array of Election Sermons.[5]

Sibley[6] says that Stoughton, Shepard, Oakes, and Torrey who preached in 1674, all exhibit in their Election sermons, "the prevalent clerical views of the day," and that "all of them have a bearing on religious toleration."   By this time there was created

---

[1] Shepard's "Eye-Salve," p. 13.   [2] *Ibid.* p. 44.

[3] Oakes's "New-England Pleaded with," p. 19.   [4] *Ibid.* p. 36.

[5] "New-England Pleaded with, And pressed to consider the things which concern her Peace, at least in this her Day: Or, A Seasonable and Serious Word of faithful Advice to the Churches and People of God (primarily those) in the *Massachusets Colony;* musingly to Ponder, and bethink themselves, what is the Tendency, and will certainly be the sad Issue, of sundry unchristian and crooked wayes, which too too many have been turning aside unto, if persisted and gone on in."

[6] Sibley's "Graduates," i. p. 328.

in New England that inevitable class of thinkers who see the glory only of the past; for them there is no sunrise, it is always sunset. To Samuel Torrey, who was one of these painful preachers, the golden age of New England, though then dating back less than forty years, was gone forever. " Truly, so it is, the very heart of *New-England* is changed, and exceedingly corrupted with the sins of the Times : there is a Spirit of Profaneness, a Spirit of Pride, a Spirit of Worldliness, a Spirit of Sensuality, a Spirit of Gainsaying and Rebellion, a Spirit of Libertinism, a Spirit of Carnality, Formality, Hypocrisie, and Spiritual Idolatry in the Worship of God." [1] A rich crop of tares considering the preciousness of the " seed corn ! " This was surely a wicked world in 1674 to contain so many evil " Spirits," yet good Mr. Torrey lingered in it long enough to preach two more Election sermons, one in 1683, and one in 1695, and died in 1707 at the ripe age of seventy-five. In his last sermon he was still taking a gloomy view and holding fast by the ministry as a forlorn hope. Yet there was in him a deep concern for the cure of souls, and his earnestness may have been as sincere as Carlyle's. At all events such men had none of that smug optimism of more recent years, which prompted a clergyman of this state, recently deceased, to pray to his Maker for " that self-complacency which is the balm of life."

Joshua Moody preached in 1675, and again in 1692 ; but neither of his sermons is known to exist in print, I am of the opinion, however, that both were printed. In connection with the first sermon is the following entry in the " Colony Records " : " This Court, considering the elaborate & seasonable discourse of the Reūend Mr Joshua Moody enterteyned the Generall Assembly with on the day of elecčon, judge meet to entreate the sajd Mr Moody to transcribe a copy thereof meete for the presse, that it may be printed." [2] Sibley says " the sermon may not have been printed." [3] An additional, though slight, reason for thinking it was printed, is that Increase Mather, in 1677, spoke of it as " that Scripture which was worthily opened and applyed in this place upon the like solemn occasion two years ago, Judg. 2. 7. 10." [4] As for the 1692 sermon, Haven's list in Thomas's " History of

[1] Torrey's Election Sermon for 1674, p. 8.
[2] Massachusetts Colony Records, v. 34.   [3] Sibley's "Graduates." i. 379.
[4] Mather's "A Call from Heaven," 1677, p. 59 ; second impression, 1685, p. 81.

Printing in America," gives the following title : " People of New England Reasoned with. Election Sermon, May 4, 1692." Samuel Sewall has an interesting entry regarding the election for 1692: " May 4. Election-Day, Major Hutchinson and Capt. Greenough's Companies attend, Mr. Moodey preaches. Dine at Wing's. . . . No Treat at the Governour's but Beer, Cider, Wine."[1]

All honor to Moody (or, as he spelt it, Moodey), for, if we may believe the Reverend William Bentley,[2] he advised those arrested on the charge of witchcraft to evade trial by running away !

The " Happiness of a People in the Wisdome of their Rulers," preached by William Hubbard in 1676, was a very long sermon, and even to Hubbard's patient contemporaries a very dry one, for the first edition does not seem to have sold well. It was printed by John Foster in 1676, not long after he had set up his press in Boston, and being a stout and solid little quarto of some seventy pages, did not create a very lively demand. There was commercial enterprise in Boston, however, from its start ; Foster bound up the unsalable sheets with Hubbard's more popular " Narrative of the Troubles with the Indians," and so, shrewdly disposed of the edition. By itself, or with the Narrative, this sermon has, of course, great bibliographical interest. Hubbard was inclined to clemency, and even went so far towards liberalism as to doubt if a heretic deserves capital punishment.[3] I regret to say that the views on the civil service expressed in this discourse were sadly corrupt. He says on this point, " Concerning inferiour Officers, such as are Fiscalls & Treasurers, whose places (by reason of the profit they usually are attended with) are more liable to temptation & corruption, there is no matter of danger in their change."[4]

Increase Mather, who may fairly be called the prince of Election preachers, appeared four times before the Court, — in 1677, 1693, 1699, and in 1702. Not only did this eminent man do what he could to perpetuate the custom, but he seemed to have had, in common with many, a genuine reverence for the entire public ceremony of which it was a part. His first sermon, that for 1677, was only printed in a larger work of his, " A Call from Heaven." In his blasts against " sinful toleration," and " Hideous clamours

1 Sewall's Diary, i. 360.
2 1 Massachusetts Historical Collections, x. 65.
3 Hubbard's " Happiness of a People," 1676, p. 39.   4 *Ibid.* p. 26.

for liberty of Conscience," he no doubt spoke with that "tonitruous cogency" for which his son tells us he was famous.

An historical interest attaches to the sermon for 1693. Mather had lately returned from his mission to England to secure the second Charter, and his discourse is in part a vindication of himself and of the Charter against some unfavorable criticism. It is commendably short, and closes with a rather faint admonition to pray for the King. "And pray for the Queen!" he adds, bringing to mind, by this afterthought, Dr. Chauncy's famous prayer for the drowned boy.

Unfortunately there is no trace of the sermon preached in 1678 by Samuel Phillips of Rowley, the great-great-great-grandfather of Wendell Phillips. The preacher showed a fondness for free speech, — which he must have transmitted, — for he was imprisoned for the "crime" of calling Randolph a "wicked man."

James Allen, who preached in 1679, admitted having "soul tremblings" at the thought of speaking on such an occasion. The typography of his sermon is strikingly good; the type is fine, and on the whole clear, while there is a noticeable absence of an excess of capital letters. Of Phillips's sermon the year before, he says : "If their missing it further your prayer, that is the best way to rectifie their proceedings, 1 Tim. 2. 1, 2, whence you were solemnly exhorted to it the last year, by a faithful Servant of Christ."[1] There is some reason to suppose, herefrom, that this discourse may have appeared in print.

Nothing more is known respecting the sermon for 1680, by Edward Bulkley, and that for 1681, by William Brimsmead, beyond the fact that both were preached.

Samuel Willard's sermon for 1682 was printed as part of a larger work, "The Child's Portion," and is entitled, "The only sure way to prevent threatened calamity." A reading of his words convinces one that he spoke the truth when he said, "I am far from pleading for or justifying anything that looks like *Enthusiasm*." Still it must be borne in mind that he abode long enough in this frail tabernacle to become the father of twenty children. He preached also in 1694, thirty-five years after graduation, on "The Character of a good Ruler;" which is, to tell the truth, the subject of four-

---

[1] Allen's Election Sermon for 1679, p. 8.

fifths of all Election Sermons. His ideas, however, were in advance of his times. " Civil Government is seated in no particular
Persons or Families by a Natural right," he says; "neither," he
continues, "hath the Light of Nature, nor the Word of God deter-
mined, what Form of Government shall be established among men,
whether *Monarchical, Aristocratical,* or *Democratical.*" [1]

There are in every generation certain persons who seem to be
especially delegated to preserve for future generations the smaller,
but not necessarily unimportant, facts of contemporary life. Such
a man was Pepys to England, and another was Judge Samuel
Sewall, the Diarist. Among the varied occupations of this good
man's life was, curiously enough, a diligent solicitude for the
preaching of and listening to the Massachusetts Election Sermons.
But for him, and the Mathers, the great collections in the Massachusetts Historical Society and the Boston Public Library could
not have existed. These men were succeeded in their tasks by the
Reverend Thomas Prince, and a century later by the Reverend
John Pierce. I shall not hesitate to quote freely from Sewall's
Diary, for I am convinced that he made these sermons his especial
care; he even interested himself in the printing of them; and he
would often present copies as tender souvenirs. In fact, he never
seemed to go abroad without one about his person. Once — to
mention a solitary instance — he meets Mr. Pemberton " by Mr.
Gerrishe's shop . . . he was going, it seems, to Madam Saltonstall's.
I went with him having Election-Sermons in my Pocket." [2]

John Hale preached in 1684; and was asked to prepare a copy
for the press. " 'This Court, taking notice of the great paynes &
labour of the Reūend Mr John Hale in his sermon vpon the last
election day, doe hereby order Samuell Nowell, Esqr, Mr Henry
Bartholmew, Capt Daniel Epps, & Mr Excercise Connant to give
Mr Hale the thanks of this Court for his great pajnes, and that, as
a further testimony of their acceptance thereof, doe in the Courts
name desire a coppy of him, that may be fitted for the presse,
and to take effectuall care that the same be printed at the publick
charge." [3]   No copy is known. Sibley says, " I have not seen a
copy of this sermon, nor the title in any catalogue." [4]   It is curious
that Sprague, in his " Annals of the American Pulpit," should

---

[1] Willard's Election Sermon for 1694, p. 20.   [2] Sewall's Diary, iii. 7.
[3] Massachusetts Colony Records, v. 441.   [4] Sibley's " Graduates," i. 519.

speak of this sermon as, with one exception, "the only product of Mr. Hale's pen, known to have been printed."[1]

"God's eye on the contrite," by William Adams, in 1685, is representative of the flagellations which the old ministers used to visit upon crying sins. "Privileged professors," he says, "may be discovered to be sinners; some to be proud, haughty, high-minded, supercilious, self-exalting, arrogant; others to be sensual, intemperate, corrupt, fleshly, lascivious; . . . others to be covetous, unjust, oppressive,"[2] and so on, even to the extent of being "company-keepers" who "sit and spend time with vain persons." "Low worms" the worthy parson finds his fellows, and "that the Great God should look upon such nothings, is a great stoop."[3] We find Mr. Adams, on 6 August of the same year, in company with Mr. Torrey, another sorrowful Election preacher, at Sewall's house. "This day his [Adams's] Election Sermon came out, and Augt. the 7th Friday morn, he gave me the Errata, which was chiefly carried *away* in stead of carried with ambition. Suped with a new sort of Fish called Coñers, my wife had bought, which occasioned Discourse on the Subject. Mr. Adams returned Thanks."[4] His sermon was reprinted in the "Dedham Pulpit." (Boston, 1840.)

Michael Wigglesworth was the preacher in 1686, and his text was from Revelation ii. 4, but no copy of the sermon seems to exist, although a request for the press was made. "It is ordered, that Mr Humphry Davy & Mr Treasurer give the Reũend Mr Michael Wigglesworth the thanks of this Court for his sermon on Wednesday last, & to desire him speedily to prepare the same for the presse, adding thereto what he had not then time to deliuer, the Court judging that the printing of it will be for publick bennefitt."[5] The preacher may not have been well enough to comply with this request, for in his prayer he speaks of his ill-health.[6] Mr. John Ward Dean's explanation of the failure of this sermon to appear is that "as the government was dissolved soon after, it is possible that the sermon was never printed, though in several lists it is marked as having been printed."[7] Mr. Sibley

---

[1] Sprague's Annals, i. 170.
[2] Adams's Election Sermon for 1685, p. 11.   [3] *Ibid.* p. 17.
[4] Sewall's Diary, i. 92.   [5] Massachusetts Colony Records, v. 514.
[6] Sewall's Diary, i. 136.
[7] Memoir of Wigglesworth, p. 93.

thinks the change in the government rendered the printing of it "inexpedient or inconvenient."[1] The "American Quarterly Register," however, states that "He preached the Election Sermon in 1686, which was published."[2]

A double interest attaches to this sermon, both because of the condition of affairs in the Colony at its delivery, and from the character of him who preached it. The following extract from Sewall's Diary is all that is likely to be known concerning it: —

"May 12, 1686. Pleasant day. Governour ill of 's Gout, goes not to Meeting. Mr. Wigglesworth preaches from Rev. 2. 4 and part of 5ᵗʰ v. and do thy first works, end of the Text. Shew'd the want of Love, or abating in it, was ground enough of Controversy, whatsoever outward performances a people might have. In 's prayer said, That may know the things of our peace in this our day, and it may be the last of our days. Acknowledged God as to the Election, and bringing forth him as 't were a dead Man, — had been reckoned among the dead, — to preach."[3]

"There are," says Hutchinson, "no public records from the dissolution of the old charter government in 1686, until the restoration of it in 1689."[4] Sewall's Diary, too, is silent regarding the sermons during this period, nor do I find any hint regarding them elsewhere. It seems, therefore, highly probable[5] that blanks must be left for the years 1687 and 1688, — the first since 1662, and the last to occur, with three exceptions, until 1885.

Like his father, Cotton Mather preached four times, if it be decided to admit in the regular series his sermon delivered at the deposition of Andros before the "Honourable Convention of the Governour, Council, and Representatives . . . on May 23, 1689." In his half religious, half superstitious manner, Mather explains the cause of the frequent evils in the Colony. But there have been monitions, too, he thinks; "Especially the Sermons which our Elections have put the Embassadours of God upon *Preaching* and *Printing* of; these have so many loud *Warnings* unto us."[6]

[1] Sibley's "Graduates," i. 285.   [2] American Quarterly Register, xi. 193.

[3] Sewall's Diary, i. 136.

[4] History of Massachusetts-Bay, i. 354, *note*.

[5] "Not till after the deposition of Gov. Andros, I presume, was another Election Sermon preached at Boston." (Dean's Memoir of Wigglesworth, p. 92.)

[6] Mather's "Way to Prosperity," p. 23.

Characteristically, he smuggles in something entirely foreign to the subject; this time it is a " *Discourse* fetch't from a *Reserved* Collection of MEMORABLE PROVIDENCES," in which he gossips of red snow, of a wondrous cabbage with three branches, and of other marvels equally germane to the "Way to Prosperity." [1]

"Above seventy years have rolled about, since a Frenchman," — in this decidedly modern and romantic manner Cotton Mather begins his sermon, "The Serviceable Man," for 1690. He deals with the Andros government as it deserved; calls the Quakers " the most *Malicious*, as well as the most *Pernicious* Enemies," [2] and dubs some of the contentious New Englanders "silly chickens." He mentions one person in the General Court "who can count, I suppose, Threescore years from the Time that first he took a seat among our *Magistrates* " [3] — meaning, no doubt, the venerable Bradstreet. It was a lively sermon, and in many respects "sensible," as we now understand the word.

Cotton Mather's Sermon for 1696 is one of the two needed to complete the printed series in possession of the Massachusetts Historical Society. Copies of this rare work are owned by the American Antiquarian Society of Worcester, and by the Boston Public Library.[4] In connection with the occasion of its delivery Sewall has the following entry: " May 27, 1696. Election. Rainy day, which wet the Troops that waited on the Lieut. Governour to Town. Mr. Cotton Mather preaches. Powring out Water at Mispeh, the Text." [5]

The ill-printed sermon for 1700, " A Pillar of Gratitude," was Cotton Mather's last effort at the Annual election. It is full of such naïveté as the following : " Indeed New England is not Heaven. That we are sure of! But for my part, I do not ask to

---

[1] The imprint of some copies of this sermon, "The Way to Prosperity," is : Boston, Printed by Richard Pierce, for Benjamin Harris, Anno Domini, 1690; of other copies it is : Printed by R. Pierce, for Joseph Brunning, Obadiah Gill, and James Woode. (See Sibley's " Graduates," iii. 50.) This sermon may also be found in Cotton Mather's " Wonderful Works of God commemorated."

[2] Mather's Election Sermon for 1690, p. 34.   [3] *Ibid.* p. 58.

[4] The title is: "Things for a Distress'd People to think upon." There was an imperfect copy in George Brinley's library, which lacked three pages of the Postscript. The Worcester copy includes only pp. 5–74. The only known perfect copy is in the Boston Public Library. These three are the only copies of which I have heard.

[5] Sewall's Diary, i. 426.

remove out of New-England, except for a Removal unto Heaven." [1]
Here is a spark of early Know-Nothingism : "At length it was
proposed, that a colony of Irish might be sent over, to check the
growth of this countrey: an Happy Revolution spoiled that
Plot." [2]

No preacher is known for 1691, nor can I find any explanation
for this omission, as in the cases of the years 1687, 1688, 1752,
and 1764.

Mr. Edes has put in brackets the Christian name, John, of the
Reverend Mr. Danforth who preached in 1697; but there is really
no doubt that the preacher was John Danforth of Dorchester, who,
Sibley says, "preached the Artillery Election Sermon in 1693,
and the Election Sermon in 1697; but they may not have been
printed." [3] Sewall's entry for 26 May, 1697, is : "Election day :
Capt. Foster Guards the Governour to the Town-house, where the
Court had a Treat. Mr. Danforth preaches. Dine at the stone
house." [4] Later on, in 1707, Sewall makes a memorandum, which
settles all doubt, as follows: "Tuesday, Jany 14th. Govr calls a
Council, Propounds Mr. Danforth, Dorchester, and Mr. Belchar
of Newbury to Preach the Election Sermon; Mr. Samuel Belchar
is agreed on, Mr. Danforth having preach'd before." [5] On the same
page Sewall speaks of giving away several copies of Higginson's
Election Sermon.

The memory of Nicholas Noyes, who preached in 1698, is not a

---

[1] Mather's Election Sermon for 1700, p. 11.   [2] *Ibid.* p. 31.
[3] Sibley's " Graduates," ii. 514.
[4] Sewall's Diary, i. 453. This was the Star Tavern. It stood on the north-
easterly corner of Hanover and Union streets, running back to and abutting
upon Link Alley (later known as North Federal Court), which was discontinued,
closed, and built upon in 1857–1860. It was here that the Court of Admiralty
sat, in 1704, for the trial of Capt. John Quelch and his company for piracy,
when Stephen North was the inn-keeper. Cf. Sewall's Diary, ii. 108; Province
Laws, viii. 395, *note;* Shurtleff's Topographical and Historical Description of
Boston, pp. 405, 607, 630, 656; Nomenclature of Streets (Boston City Document No. 119 of 1879), pp. 21, 26, 35, 89, 95; John Bonner's Plan of 1722;
John Groves Hales's Maps of the Street Lines of Boston in 1819 and 1820,
p. 185; and Annual Report of the Boston Street Laying Out Department for
1894 (City Document No. 35 of 1895), pp. 196, 228.
I am indebted to Mr. Henry H. Edes for this valuable note, which identifies
not only the "Stone House," but a lost alley.
[5] Sewall's Diary, ii. 178.

sweet savor in New-England history. He was not only a prosecutor at witch-trials, but also a punster and a writer of obituary poetry; notwithstanding all this, there is reason to suppose him to have been a God-fearing, and in most respects a good, man. He finally confessed his madness towards witches, and sought to repair the evil done. He fell into the fashion of his age and of his cloth in preaching the "degeneracy of the times." In his sermon of ninety-nine pages he draws up his indictments, — irreligion, swearing, and so on, sixteen counts in all, — against his country. Yet, he admits, " it cannot with truth be asserted, that as yet we are as bad as bad can be ; for there is real danger of growing worse." [1] He also seriously discourses as to whether Indians are really worth converting ! [2] There is at the end of the sermon an interesting short account of the plantations of Indians in the Province, written by "preachers to the Indians in their own tongue," — Grindall Rawson and Samuel Danforth, both of whom preached Election Sermons later. This mournful Noyes grew " very corpulent," and is said to have died choked with blood from the curse of a witch ; this end was meted out with a justice more poetical than his obituary verses, for he would not on one occasion pray with John Procter, a condemned witch, when even their dinner had been taken from the poor witch's children by the sheriff.[3] More humane to children than Noyes was Michael Wigglesworth with his liberal eagerness to grant infants in another life " the easiest room in hell."

I have dwelt upon the Election Sermons for the Seventeenth century at length, for they are interesting chiefly because of their age ; there is, furthermore, such uncertainty regarding the existence of some of them in printed form, that any account of them is important. Moreover, there were giants in those days, — the two Shepards, Mitchel, Higginson, Norton, Oakes, the Mathers, far as their teachings seem removed from the humane ideas of later times, were mighty men ; their sermons, full of a parade of theology, overburdened with Scriptural quotations and too frequent expressions of the fear, common to the clergy, of degeneracy, were, nevertheless, masterly. As I have said, Shepard's " Eye-Salve " for 1672 is worthy of being regarded a New England classic.

---

[1] Noyes's Election Sermon for 1698, p. 58.   [2] Ibid. pp. 69 et seq.
[3] Samuel G. Drake's " The Witchcraft Delusion in New England," iii. 40.

I shall not attempt to describe particularly the Election Sermons of the eighteenth century; several good collections of them exist, and may without much difficulty be consulted. There is, moreover, little variety in the treatment of subjects appropriate to election-day; it will be found also, even among election preachers, that there were some, troubled with the modern complaint of "mental absorption," who repeated other preachers' ideas. For a hundred years after Mitchel's famous "Nehemiah on the Wall," the favorite prototype of the exemplary ruler was Nehemiah; he was served up to suit every palate. He disappeared from the Election Sermons after the Revolution, though I have noticed a tendency to resuscitate him as late as 1850. It would hardly be possible to say how many times one is reminded in these discourses that rulers are "nursing fathers of the State," or "God's vicegerents here on earth." Like the character of Nehemiah such phrases became part of the preacher's stock of ideas.

In 1701, Sewall writes, under the date of 28 May, "Mr. Cooke, Addington, Walley, and self goe in my Coach and meet the Lieut Gov.; met the Guard and his Honor near the first Brook. Mr. Belchar[1] preaches; Lt Govr, notwithstanding his Infirmities, was an Auditor."[2]

Harvard College was much in the prayers and sermons of these older divines; the College certainly had its ups and downs — more often perhaps being in sore straits, now wanting money, now pupils. Judging from some passages in these sermons, I do not think there was exaggeration in an old account of a visit to the College[3] where the narrator found "eight or ten young fellows, sitting around, smoking tobacco." Solomon Stoddard, in his sermon for 1703, says, "'tis not worth the while for persons to be sent to the *Colledge* to learn to Complement men, and Court Women; they should be sent thither to prepare them for Publick Service, and had need be under the over-sight of wise and holy men."[4] It was Stoddard who preached until his eighty-sixth year without the use of notes.[5]

---

[1] This was Joseph Belcher; Samuel Belcher preached in 1707.

[2] Sewall's Diary. ii. 34.

[3] Journal by Dankers and Sluyter (Memoirs, Long Island Historical Society, i.), p. 385.

[4] Stoddard's Election Sermon for 1703, p. 13.

[5] Sibley's "Graduates," ii. 114.

Jonathan Russell — whom Sewall calls "an Orthodox Usefull Man "[1] — says in 1704, in a rather gloomy if slangy manner, "we han't Glorifyed God as God, nor been thankful."[2] On the other hand, the next year, Joseph Estabrook, in his "Abraham the Passenger," says, " I believe there are as many real Saints in this Land as in any Land or Nation in the World, for the quantity of People."[3] In this year, 1705, Governor Joseph Dudley, in one of his half-insane freaks, tried to disallow the right of the election of a Speaker by the House. The election exercises went on, however. Sewall says: " Now t' was Candle-Lighting; for went into Meetinghouse about 12. Mr. Easterbrooks made a very good Sermon."[4] The next day Sewall continues: " Brown, Sewall, Lynde go to thank Mr. Easterbrooks for his Sermon and desire a copy : He Thanks the Gov[r] and Council for their Acceptance of his mean Labours and shews his unwillingness to be in print."[5]

John Rogers of Ipswich preached in 1706, notwithstanding that the year before the Legislature had ordered two pamphlets sent them by this preacher and Rev. Mr. Rogers of Boxford, " to be burnt by the common hangman, near the whipping-post in Boston."[6] The act was no doubt a phase of the contention between Dudley and the House.

In 1708 there seems to have existed disaffection in the minds of some, and among them of Cotton Mather, concerning the government, upon which it is not worth while to dwell ; John Norton of Hingham, however, " preaches a Flattering Sermon as to the Governour"[7] in which he speaks of "this Great and Good Assembly, an Assembly of chosen People of the Lord."

"May 25 [1709]," Sewall says, "At Wiñisimet overtook Mr. Corwin, went over together; got to Boston about ten. Heard Mr. Rawson preach the Election Sermon — Before your feet stumble upon the dark Mountains."[8] We may hope confidently that Sewall heard the text with profit, and did not permit his feet to stumble, for the next entry is " Dine at the Green Dragon." This sermon

---

[1] Sewall's Diary, ii. 301.
[2] Russell's Election Sermon for 1704, p. 11.
[3] Estabrook's Election Sermon for 1705, p. 16.
[4] Sewall's Diary, ii. 132.   [5] Ibid. ii. 132.
[6] Sibley's "Graduates," iii. 273.   [7] Sewall's Diary, ii. 224.
[8] Ibid. ii. p. 256.

mentions the death of a famous New England trio, Torrey, Willard, and Higginson, and comments on the "tricks and shifts " of towns to evade the school laws. It was a sturdy old discourse of forty closely printed pages, divided into four propositions, each in turn subdivided and rounded off with an application and exhortation.

A little unpleasantness was prefatory to the delivery of Ebenezer Pemberton's sermon in 1710. Samuel May of Wrentham wrote two letters refusing to preach, and after some discussion Mr. Pemberton was agreed on. Sewall says, " Then Mr. Secretary did the Message. Mr. Pemberton disabled himself." [1] The preacher is still coyly excusing himself, while Sewall continues, " As we look towards the Artillery passing by, I said to Mr. Pemberton the passage of Ulysses, —

' Si mea cum vestris valuissent vota Pelasgi.'

Before we went away, word was brought that Dr. Mather was chosen to preach the Artillery Sermon. Mr. Pemberton said Must choose agen." [2] A few days later the worthy man fell into a pet with Sewall, apparently because he had lost a good dinner; but the two dined together at the Green Dragon after the delivery of a sermon, which is printed in one hundred and six pages, and reprinted in his Sermons and Discourses (London, 1727). Sewall adds, " 70. before sermon." [3] This evidently means that seventy members had been already sworn in. It cannot be that the audience was no more than seventy, else Pemberton would not have spoken of appearing "this Day in this *Awful Desk*." [4]

The choice of a preacher in 1712 occasioned some debate, and finally Samuel Cheever was selected. " The Govr seem'd to decline Mr. Walter and begin to hover over Mr. Anger." [5] This, I suppose, was the Mr. Angier who, in 1710, Sewall did not think was a sufficiently "Square and Stable a Man " [6] for the honor. We learn parenthetically that, during Cheever's sermon, Sewall's son Joseph was taken with one of his " intermitting fevers."

Samuel Treat preached in 1713, but we have not the sermon.

[1] Sewall's Diary, ii. 278.   [2] *Ibid.* ii. 278.   [3] *Ibid.* ii. 282.
[4] Pemberton's Election Sermon for 1710, p. 4.
[5] Sewall's Diary, ii. 333.   [6] *Ibid.* ii. 278.

His text, according to Sewall, was Psalms ii. 8. Dr. Isaac P. Langworthy, high authority in everything relating to early New-England religious literature, was firmly of the opinion that the sermons for 1713 and 1717 were never printed, although both preachers were formally requested to prepare their productions for the press. The year 1713 was one of disturbance in Boston, for then occurred its first and only bread riot, when some two hundred people sought to find corn in Arthur Mason's storehouse on the Common. All this may have put less important matters into the background. Sibley mentions a volume of Treat's sermons " correctly transcribed and apparently designed for publication ; " [1] perhaps this sermon is therein. Treat, we learn, was a kindly man, with a loud voice, but he was a stiff Calvinist. Somewhere he cheerfully exclaims to the backslider, " Thou must erelong go to the bottomless pit. Hell hath enlarged herself, and is ready to receive thee." [2] Sewall has a few words on the lost sermon, and says that it " Encourag'd Rulers to be Faithfull ; Christ would meet them with better Revivals and Refreshm'ts than Melchizedec met Abraham with. Gave this advice as to choice of Rulers, whatever other accomplishments were ; yet, *Si profanus* is to be avoided." [3] Notwithstanding all this good advice, General Wait Still Winthrop was " dropped " at the election.

Concerning the Indians, very little appears in these sermons of this period ; and this is curious, for they and the witches occupied largely the attention of early New England. In connection, however, with this topic, Jeremiah Shepard, in his discourse for 1715, says, " A work never to be forgotten, is the Lord's preparing this wilderness for his people when he swept away thousands of those salvage Tawnies (those cursed Devil worshippers) with a mortal Plague, to make room for a better People." [4] I have not come across a more heartless Pharisaism than this.

Although in the list of preachers in Andrew Bigelow's sermon for 1836, the sermon preached by Roland Cotton in 1717 is mentioned as being of duodecimo size, there is strong reason to believe that it was never printed. Cotton was, however, asked to prepare it for the press. Sibley quotes, perhaps from Josiah

[1] Sibley's " Graduates," ii. 308. [2] *Ibid.* ii. 309.
[3] Sewall's Diary, ii. 385. [4] Shepard's Election Sermon for 1715, p. 20.

Cotton's manuscript diary, to the effect that Roland Cotton " would never suffer any of his works to come out in print." [1]

The eighteenth century was still young when protests began to be common against the condition of the finances, and particularly against the Province Bills. It is too long a story to go into here; but it is relevant to say that the Election preachers kept the low state of the credit constantly in the minds of their hearers. Benjamin Colman, who was something of a radical for those days, says plainly in 1718, " what we call a *hundred* Pounds is really but as *seventy*, if so much." [2] This subject, and the condition of the College and the "inferior" schools, were often recurred to at this period.

In 1719 Sewall mentions one of the few instances of a declination to preach. " March, 11. The Gen'l Court meets. Send in a Message that Mr. Wise declin'd preaching the Election Sermon, and they had chosen Mr. Williams of Hatfield to preach it." [3]

Election Sermons have unquestionably been instrumental for good in various ways; they have fired patriotic zeal, strengthened irresolution, perhaps consoled the sick or needy, or converted the backslider; but I do not conceive that any mortal but Samuel Sewall would ever have thought of using an Election Sermon as a philtre to excite the tender emotions of love. In his famous but unsuccessful suit to Mrs. Ruggles, after the death of his first wife, on one occasion he " went in the Coach and visited Mrs. Ruggles after Lecture. . . . Made some Difficulty to accept an Election Sermon, lest it should be an obligation on her." [4] Later, he says, " I gave her [the same lady] Mr. Moodey's Election Sermon [for 1721] Marbled, with her name written in it." [5]

It may be mentioned incidentally that in Colman's sermon for 1723 is an interesting notice of Thomas Hollis and of his gifts to the College.

Joseph Sewall, son of the Diarist, preached in 1724. His views of what Sunday-keeping ought to be seem strict even for those strait-laced days. " And is not the Evil Custom of keeping open Shops on the Evening before the Day, a Prophanation of the Sab-

[1] Sibley's " Graduates," iii. 325.
[2] Colman's Election Sermon for 1718, p. 40.
[3] Sewall's Diary, iii. 214.   [4] *Ibid.* iii. 291.
[5] *Ibid.* iii. 291.

bath, which ought to be Reform'd?"[1] He attacks some of the
darling sins of that age, rebuking even the "*attending of Funerals
when no present Necessity requires it.*"[2] In 1727, Joseph Baxter
asks, "May not something be done to prevent unnecessary Jour-
neyings on the Lord's-Day?"[3] "A Formal Laodicean Indiffer-
ency," and other symptoms of the degeneracy of the age, was the
subject of Ebenezer Thayer's discourse in 1725. Sewall says,
"Election-Day, good Wether. Went in to the L[t] Governour's
Treat . . . Mr. Thayer preaches from Jer. 6, 8. — Be instructed O
Jerusalem. Dine at the Exchange Tavern . . . I was sick of the
Election."[4] Though growing old, Sewall still maintains his interest in the Election Sermon. A little earlier in the same year
he writes, "I left 3 Election Sermons and 3 of Mr. Mayhew's
Lecture Sermons with Capt. Phips."[5]

Some of the words and phrases used by these early preachers
have interested and amazed me. What congregation to-day could
understand such words as "epanalepsis," "horrendous," and
"aposiopesis"? Extremely simple language also, colloquialisms,
and even ungrammatical expres ions are frequent. In Breck's
sermon (1728) we find "brizzils" for bristles.[6] Samuel Fiske (1731)
speaks of "the bear reading of the Psalm."[7] Many unusual
words or phrases may be due to errors of the press, not of the
preacher. Linguistically, few sermons are more entertaining than
that stiff and pedantic one by John Swift of Framingham in
1732, who is much alarmed at certain "*Horribilia de Deo ;*" one
of which is that "some would induce us to believe that Hell-fire
is shortly and in some time to be quench'd, or that the Torments
of Hell are not everlasting."[8] Harvard College he calls "that
Primrose of all His Majesty's Dominions in *America.*"[9]

Of Thomas Prince's valuable discourse for 1731, nothing need
be said, except that in the Appendix is reprinted a long extract

---

[1] Sewall's Election Sermon for 1724, p. 65.   [2] *Ibid.* p. 66.
[3] Baxter's Election Sermon for 1727, p. 32.
[4] Sewall's Diary, iii. 356.
[5] *Ibid.* iii. 348.
[6] Breck's Election Sermon for 1728, p. 22.
[7] Fiske's Election Sermon for 1731, p. 10.
[8] Swift's Election Sermon for 1732, p. 23.
[9] *Ibid.* p. 25.

from Stoughton's sermon for 1668. Prince suggests, furthermore that "the Excellent Election Sermons of Mr. Higginson, Mitchel, Stoughton, Danforth, Shepard, Oakes, Torrey, &c. . . . might be of Publick Service were they Reprinted and Dispersed." [1]

By numerous implications, it may be assumed not only that the annual delivery of the sermon was a matter of general interest, but also that it was well attended. Samuel Wigglesworth (1733) speaks of the " Vast Assembly." This Mr. Wigglesworth is watchful of the follies of his generation, particularly of its " Exorbitant Reach after riches."

A tendency of preachers to be lachrymose is remarked by Edward Holyoke in 1736, who says, " In the choice of this Subject, I vary from many of my Fathers and superior Brethren, who (before me) have stood in this Desk upon the like Occasion, in that they have chosen to discourse of the Apostacy of this People of God, and drop their tears over their Immoralities." [2] But the next year Israel Loring makes a rather sour rejoinder, and dwells fondly on the congenial theme " of the Degeneracies, that the People of the Land are fallen into." [3] It seems that then as now neglect of public duties was especially due to " Light Indispositions of Body, small Difficulties of the Weather, and Distance of the Way." [4] Loring may be pardoned his platitudes, for he makes the creditable suggestion that the descendants of the victims of the witchcraft persecutions be in some way indemnified for injury or disgrace. [5] Lest he should here have shown too liberal a disposition, he advises in conclusion a more frequent " preaching up the Doctrine of Hell-torments." [6] Amid all these comminations of the wickedness of the age, I notice no censure of slavery.

The sermons continue to be outspoken in regard to the finances of the Province. In 1738 John Webb speaks of the fluctuating state of "our Medium of Trade," — meaning, of course, the paper currency. Charles Chauncy, in the appendix to his important sermon for 1747, quotes the views of John Barnard and Nathaniel Appleton, and refers with candor to the evil condition of the cur-

[1] Prince's Election Sermon for 1731, p. 37.
[2] Holyoke's Election Sermon for 1736, p. 6.
[3] Loring's Election Sermon for 1737, p. 1.   [4] Ibid. p. 12.
[5] Ibid. p. 51.   [6] Ibid. p. 60.

rency and the public bills, especially so far as this subject directly affected the ministers.[1] In 1749 William Balch refers to "Our wretched Paper-medium." Finally, in 1751, William Welsteed is able to congratulate the public on a deliverance from the "Iniquitous medium," which took place in 1750.

Up to the period of the French and Indian wars the Province had for some time been enjoying immunity from political disturbance, and as a result the clergy had to fall back on such old and well-worn themes as the inviolability of Charter rights, or ply the scourge over social and moral evils. Mr. John Webb in 1738, Mr. William Williams in 1741, Mr. Nathaniel Appleton in 1742, all speak strongly on the matter of the Charter; the proximity in point of time of the several sermons on this subject would seem to show that just then some especial danger was apprehended in this direction, or it may have been a manifestation of the Congregational party thus early putting itself on guard against the slow, almost motionless advance of the English hierarchy toward America. This is overtly alluded to in Chauncy's sermon for 1747, when he remarks, " But justice in rulers should be seen likewise in their care of the *religious* rights and liberties of a people. Not that they are to exert their authorities in *settling articles of faith*, or *imposing modes of worship*." [2] Notwithstanding such open opinions, there was not much in these sermons which appears to foreshadow the coming Revolution. The clergy, as usual, were conservative as long as possible ; and the people no doubt approved Mr. Cooper's sentiment, in his sermon for 1740, that " The Notion of *Levelism* has as little Foundation in Nature as in Scripture," [3] and that it was better " to *pray more* for Rulers, and *talk less* against them." [4] The next year, 1741, William Williams of Weston, occupies the safer ground of moral instruction, and inveighs against " Horse trading," "stroling about," and other dangers to the social fabric.[5]

Charles Chauncy's fearless address, in addition to its freedom from the ordinary commonplaces of Election day regard-

[1] See the Memorial of the Chaunceys, by William Chauncey Fowler, on the attitude of the General Court in this matter.

[2] Chauncy's Election Sermon for 1747, p. 36.

[3] Cooper's Election Sermon for 1740, p. 6.

[4] *Ibid.* p. 9.

[5] Williams's Election Sermon for 1741, p. 49.

ing the virtues of Nehemiah and the "nursing fathers" of the Province, had the additional merit of being well printed, and almost modern in a far less frequent use of capital letters than was in vogue then. This latter oddity I am at a loss to explain.

In the opinion of Samuel Phillips, whose sermon for 1750 affords several glimpses at contemporary affairs, the country was "exceeding all others in costly Fashions ; and for Extravagance in manner of Living." [1]

It is reasonably certain that there was no sermon preached either in 1752 or 1764, for in both those years small-pox raged in Boston.[2]

There are now dim forebodings of the democratic uprising soon to shake off the tyrannical hand, the pressure of which for a long time has not been heavy, but yet steadily increasing. Through the sermon of John Cotton of Newton in 1753 is heard the "Cry of Unrighteousness, Oppression and Extortion " [3] in the land. It was a melancholy discourse, not at all like that in 1754 by the still young Jonathan Mayhew, who had been graduated only ten years. Mayhew is bold, fearless, even aggressive. " To say the least," urges he, "monarchical government has no better foundation in the oracles of God, than any other." [4]   And again, "It is very strange we should be told, at this time of day, that loyalty and slavery mean the same thing." [5]   He constantly urges "the union of these colonies ; " has his hit at the French ; and wishes to convert the Indians,[6] whom he sees more and more coming under the control of the missionaries of the Roman Church. He dislikes the importation of foreigners, even of Protestants. Of Harvard College he frankly says: " The state of our College

---

[1] Phillips's Election Sermon for 1750, p. 42.

[2] "There were but three sessions of the General Court this year [1752]. The first session was held in Concord, on account of the small-pox which then prevailed in Boston. On the fifth of June the Assembly was prorogued to September 27th (16th, Old Style), but was again prorogued, by proclamation, August 28th, to meet at Harvard College on the twenty-second of November following." — *Province Laws*, iii. 662, note.

[3] Cotton's Election Sermon for 1753, p. 16.

[4] Mayhew's Election Sermon for 1754, p. 5.   [5] *Ibid.* p. 20.

[6] See Dr. Joseph H. Allen's Remarks upon the relations of the Mayhew family to the Indians of Martha's Vineyard, at the February, 1895, Meeting, iii. 45, *post*. See also Foote's Annals of King's Chapel, ii. 252, 253.

can neither be forgotten, nor enough lamented. . . . Indeed, if literature and the muses chiefly haunted where poverty resides — But this is a thread-bare topic." [1]

Although Samuel Checkley preached in 1755, Thomas Smith of Portland had been previously offered and had declined the honor. In his Journal he says: "I received a letter from the secretary informing me that the Governour and Council had warned me to preach the Election sermon." [2]

An anxiety consequent upon the progress of the French and Indian war was seen in the sermons of the day. Some sermons were courageous, and in some — as, for instance, in that of Ebenezer Pemberton (the second of that name who preached) in 1757 — fear was plainly expressed. At last, in 1761, Benjamin Stevens's sermon on " Liberty " celebrates the " entire conquest of Canada." [3] Within fifteen years of the Revolution, it is strange to read the words of a preacher extolling George III. as " a Prince possessed of . . . amiable virtues and excellent accomplishments," who will "protect his faithful subjects in the greatest of human blessings, the secure enjoyment of their civil and religious Rights." [4]

The rambling, chaotic ninety-three pages of which Thomas Frink delivered himself in 1758 would be tedious indeed were it not for the peculiarities of the preacher, who must have been an original. He covers sixty pages in getting to his subject, William III. The style is mystical, the sermon full of references to " viols," the " millennium," and the Second Advent. Election day, in his Scriptural language, is " the happy Day on which the Tribes of the Lord, the Heads of the Tribes, . . . assemble in the City of our Solemnities." [5] Again he rhapsodizes, " Oh Boston! thy Beauty is faded — the Lord hath taken from thee — the Judge, the Prudent, and the Ancient, the Honourable Man, and the Councellor — Help Lord, for the godly Man ceaseth — and where is the Man to be found among you to stand in the Gap?" [6] This refers to Secretary Josiah Willard, who died in 1756, and was succeeded by Secretary Oliver.

This pretentious discourse was followed in the next year, 1759,

[1] Mayhew's Election Sermon for 1754, p. 28.
[2] Thomas Smith's Journal (Willis's edition, 1849), p. 159.
[3] Stevens's Election Sermon for 1761, p. 6.   [4] Ibid. p. 57.
[5] Frink's Election Sermon for 1758, p. 1.   [6] Ibid. p. 85.

by a brief, colorless, but wholly irreproachable, effort by Joseph Parsons.

Abraham Williams, in 1762, speaks boldly of "all men being naturally equal," and mentions "Attempts of domestic Traitors, arbitrary bigotted Tyrants." [1] It is significant that the titlepage does not mention either governor or lieutenant-governor, as it was the almost invariable custom to do up to that time. Needless to say, Williams did not receive the honor of a reprint in London, as did Andrew Eliot in 1765. Eliot praised the British Constitution as the most perfect form of civil government. Of Bernard he speaks highly, but refers to Acts passed "that seem hard on the Colonies." [2] He furthermore asserts that "there is perhaps not a man to be found among us, who would wish to be independent on our mother-country." [3] He attributed most of the prevailing trouble to excessive drinking.[4]

What the good ruler ought to do is so elaborately set forth by Ebenezer Bridge, in 1767, that he would seem to be referring to Bernard. Daniel Shute, in 1768, on the other hand, was conservative, and meant to be conciliatory; but in the next year Jason Haven remarks that "Mutual confidences and affection, between Great-Britain and these Colonies, I speak it with grief, seems to be in some measure lost." [5] In this year, 1769, Joseph Jackson had been asked to preach and had declined.

Down to the period immediately preceding the Revolution, the Election Sermons for many years (and this was true of them for some years before they were discontinued) had been preached perfunctorily, if ably. The time had come when they were to play an active part, and the spoken word from the political pulpit was to help sway men's decisions. Soon after 1766 the Governor found himself without friendly support of the Council, which as fast as possible was filled by men favorable to the coming order of things. It is unnecessary here to explain the effort to

---

[1] Williams's Election Sermon for 1762, p. 19.

[2] Eliot's Election Sermon for 1765, p. 52.   [3] *Ibid.* p. 53.

[4] This is the Andrew Eliot whose Letters to Thomas Hollis (3 Massachusetts Historical Collections, iv. 398–461) are so well known for their value among pre-revolutionary documents. See other similar letters of his in Massachusetts Historical Society's Proceedings, xvi. 281 *et seq.*

[5] Haven's Election Sermon for 1769, p. 48.

secure a royally-appointed Council which should side with the
Governor. This objectionable scheme was agreed to by the Ministry in 1774; but affairs were then *præter curam*. The Governor's power of appointment of military officers, and of judicial
officers with the consent of the Council, and his power of negation
of all others chosen by the General Court were conferred in the
charter of 1691. Moreover, the people and the clergy were
jealous for all the religious privileges which had been nominally
granted them. The clergy certainly had not forgotten that, on
the restoration of Charles II., four Commissioners, of whom any
two or three were to be a quorum, had been appointed to look out
for "the reputation and credit of the Christian religion" in New
England.[1] James's man, Andros, followed this Commission, and
henceforth there was more or less of this "looking up" of the political as well as of the religious interests of the English hierarchy.
Hints of this subtle influence of a force working contrary to the
well-established religious interests of New England are not wanting, to one who reads aright, throughout these sermons. Something more tangible than hints appears in the sermons by Charles
Chauncy and by Jonathan Mayhew, especially in that one by
the latter, on the death of Charles I. William Gordon intelli-
gently explains the position of the Election preachers on this
matter as follows: "The ministers of New England being mostly
congregational, are from that circumstance, in a professional way
more attached and habituated to the principles of liberty than
if they had spiritual superiors to lord it over them, and were in
hopes of possessing in their turn, through the gift of government,
the seat of power. They oppose arbitrary rule in civil concerns
from the love of freedom, as well as from a desire of guarding
against its introduction into religious matters."[2] What Gordon
says is particularly interesting and important; for it is, so far as
I know, the first recognition of any historic value in the Election Sermon. "To the Pulpit, the Puritan Pulpit, we owe the

[1] Thornton's Pulpit of the American Revolution, p. 175.
No one has probed more cautiously or more accurately to discover the atti-
tude of the hierarchy previous to the Revolution, than has the Hon. Mellen
Chamberlain in several of his publications, but particularly in his Address on
"John Adams."
[2] History of the Revolution, i. 418, 419.

moral force which won our Independence," remarks Thornton,[1] who does full justice to the ability and courage of the ministry, and has included in his work several of the strongest discourses of this series.

Concerning the theoretical principles of political science, there is a remarkable unanimity among the patriotic sermons at the period of the Revolution and also among those for a few preceding years. All bear the unmistakable traces of Locke's Essay on Civil Government. Certain it is that for some time the preachers, almost without exception, had been expressing belief in the natural equality of man, and in the human origin of all forms of government, though generally ending their arguments with an apostrophe to the glories of the British Constitution. The precise expression, "All men are born free and equal," was inserted in the Massachusetts Declaration of Rights of 1780 by Judge John Lowell, but the idea involved therein was not infrequently expressed in these Sermons. That of Samuel Cooke for 1770 contains the essential doctrines of the Declaration of Rights and of the Revolution. Thornton reprints it with the title, "The True Principles of Civil Government." This preacher, who afterward delivered a sermon on the battle-field at Lexington in 1777, for "a Memorial of the Bloody Tragedy, barbarously acted, by a party of British Troops," was obliged to deliver his Election Sermon at Cambridge,[2] and not at the usual place, — the Town House, or probably by that time the Old South meeting-house, in Boston. This was, no doubt, as Thornton says, by reason of a "show of despotism;" but it did not intimidate the speaker from referring to the multiplying of "lucrative offices," and to subordinate offices "made the surest step to wealth and ease."[3] He refers to the disclosure by Agent Bollan of the correspondence[4] with the ministry, and calls the Charter, not "an act of grace, but a compact."[5] Of Cooke's words Thornton says: "Governor Hutchinson cannot

---

[1] Pulpit of the American Revolution, p. xxxviii.

[2] At the "Meeting-House. . . . After Divine Service the Procession returned to Harvard-Hall, where an Entertainment was provided." — *Massachusetts Gazette*, 4 June, 1770.

[3] Cooke's Election Sermon for 1770, p. 16.

[4] *Ibid.* p. 20.

[5] *Ibid.* p. 33.

have listened to this sermon, and its implied parallel of the times of Andros with his own official period, without discomfort and perhaps regret." [1] The Revolution was not yet ripe, even in the imagination of the fearless minister, who concludes with the assurance that the people "glory in the British constitution, and are abhorrent, to a man, of the most distant thought of withdrawing their allegiance from their gracious Sovereign, and becoming an independent state." [2]

In this year, besides this regular ceremony at Cambridge, there was an independent meeting at Boston before which Charles Chauncy preached. Chauncy's sermon is included in the first published list of the Election Sermons in 1794. Its title explains the reason of its delivery.[3]

John Tucker preached at Cambridge in 1771, and was more conservative in his remarks than his immediate predecessor. He refers, however, to the "absurd and exploded doctrines of passive obedience, and non-resistance." [4] Again, it is insinuated that just rulers are "not apt, in a pet, to desert the common cause." [5] The old observance of directly addressing the Governor at the close of the sermon was carried out this year, "tho' it has not been the standing custom of late." [6] In the earlier days the ministry also were formally addressed and exhorted, just after the address to the Governor and Lieutenant-Governor.

"There is not, I suppose, a native of this Province, who does not bear unfeigned loyalty to King George *the third*," [7] exclaimed Moses Parsons in his sermon for 1772. Some grievances are ad-

---

[1] Pulpit of the American Revolution, p. 177.

[2] Cooke's Election Sermon for 1770, p. 45.

[3] Trust in God, the Duty of a People in a Day of Trouble. A sermon preached, May 30th, 1770. At the request of a great number of Gentlemen, friends to the LIBERTIES of North America, who were desirous, notwithstanding the removal of the Massachusetts General-Court (unconstitutionally as they judged) to CAMBRIDGE, that GOD might be acknowledged in that house of worship at BOSTON, in which our tribes, from the days of our fathers, have annually sought to him for direction, previous to the choice of his Majesty's Council. By Charles Chauncy, D.D. Boston: printed by Daniel Kneeland, for Thomas Leverett, in Corn-Hill. 1770.

[4] Tucker's Election Sermon for 1771, p. 19. [5] *Ibid.* p. 45.

[6] *Ibid.* p. 26.

[7] Parsons's Election Sermon for 1772, p. 23.

mitted by him, to whom it seemed that the "day is become gloomy and dark, and the waters are troubled."[1] In the midst of these disturbed elements, the preacher for 1773, the Rev. Charles Turner, found time to cry out against "the immoral practice of gaming with lucrative purposes, chiefly common among persons in that which they call high life." "Amazing profanity, especially in maritime places,"[2] is likewise condemned.

In 1774, for the last time in these annals, the annual sermon was delivered before "His Excellency," then, of course, Gage, and before "the Honorable His Majesty's Council." Gad Hitchcock, the preacher, was the first, I believe, to mention the "American cause."[3] He, too, held that "In a state of nature men are equal."[4] Some courage must have been requisite to speak as he did of "wicked rulers, such as Nero, and others of later date."[5] The tardy determination of the Ministry to have a royally appointed Council is firmly met by this patriot. Choice of Council, he declares, is "a privilege, which we never have forfeited, and we are resolved we never will."[6]

A reprint of this interesting sermon was made in 1885 at the expense of the great-granddaughter of Gad Hitchcock, Mrs. Abby L. (Hitchcock) Tyler, of which only a few copies were struck off.

It has been customary to say that there were two Election Sermons preached in 1775 — one by Samuel Langdon,[7] President of Harvard, "Before the Honorable Congress of the Colony of the Massachusetts-Bay . . . Assembled at Watertown, 31st Day of May, 1775. Being the Anniversary fixed by CHARTER for the Election of Counsellors;" the other by William Gordon, the historian of the Revolution, "before the Honorable House of Representatives, on the Day intended for the Choice of Counsellors, Agreeable to the Advice of the Continental Congress," on 19 July, 1775. Langdon's sermon is doubtless to be considered as belong-

---

[1] Parsons's Election Sermon for 1772. p. 17.
[2] Turner's Election Sermon for 1773, p. 41.
[3] Hitchcock's Election Sermon for 1774, p. 45.
[4] *Ibid.* p. 20.   [5] *Ibid.* p. 13.
[6] *Ibid.* p. 42.
[7] There have been two reprints of Langdon's sermon, — one in Thornton's Pulpit of the American Revolution, and the other in "The Patriot Preachers of the American Revolution," 1860.

ing to the regular series. It was delivered at the time usual to this ceremony, and was sent, by special vote, to each minister in the Colony, and to each member of the Congress. Of it Gage said: " To complete the horrid prophanation of terms and of ideas, the name of God has been introduced in the pulpit to excite and justify devastation and massacre." [1]

Langdon was a violent Whig, but not popular as a man or as President of the College.[2] In this sermon he asserts that blood was shed at Lexington while the inhabitants "were actually complying with the command to disperse." [3] He also echoes the accusation common at that time that an attempt was making to establish Popery in the British dominions.[4]

Gordon's sermon [5] held that the war, as a means of establishing liberty, was a punishment for the moral delinquencies of the colonies, which might have separated peacefully had they been worthier. His patriotism, however, was undoubted, when he remarks, "No member can consistently take his place, or be admitted to sit in the house of Assembly, who *hesitates* about setting up government." [6] Gordon spoke again, on 4 July, 1777, before the General Court, although Samuel Webster preached regularly at the Election in that year.

Most of the sermons of this time are noticeable for directness and simplicity, in sharp contrast with the fine theorizing and theologizing of many of the earlier efforts; but Samuel West, in 1776, "before the Honorable Council," delivered a long and rather ponderous apology for the state of affairs. Although his reasoning was too abstruse for the occasion, his patriotism was sound; he even enunciated the democratic idea that the popular judgment is always right.[7] West's sermon was preached at the Old Brick meeting-house, on the site which had been dedicated to the worship of God ever since 1640.[8]

[1] Quoted by Thornton, p. 255, *note.*
[2] Patriot Preachers, p. 50.
[3] Langdon's Election Sermon for 1775, p. 8.
[4] *Ibid.* pp. 28, 29.
[5] This sermon bears the imprint, "Watertown: printed and sold by Benjamin Edes. 1775."
[6] Gordon's Sermon of 19 July, 1775, p. 27.
[7] West's Election Sermon for 1776, p. 27.
[8] This site is now (1891) occupied by the Rogers Building.

Samuel Webster, in 1777, said, among other excellent things, " Let elections of the *Legislators* be *frequent* ; Let *monopolies*, and all *kinds* and degrees of *oppression* be carefully guarded against." [1]

John Adams has plainly declared that all men in the American Revolution were not heroes; so, too, in 1778, the Reverend Samuel Phillips Payson speaks of the small contemporary criticism busy in his hearing. " The growls of avarice and curses of clowns, will generally be heard, when the public liberty and safety call for more generous and costly exertions." [2] Thus early he proposes that the General Assembly " form and establish upon generous principles a society of arts and sciences." [3]

The liberalizing tendency of the great contest can be seen even in the relatively slight matter of according the honor of delivering the Election Sermon, an honor which hitherto had seldom gone outside of Congregational ranks. In 1779, Samuel Stillman, preacher of the First Baptist Church in Boston, was chosen. He urged strongly a Bill of Rights, and maintained the " natural equality of all men." [4] His doctrine was sturdily democratic, and conceded only temporal power to all magistrates, and would seem not to have favored what is now somewhat cantingly termed putting " God in the Constitution."

For the last time before the " Honorable Council " the regular Election Sermon was preached by Simeon Howard in 1780. Although in the midst of an eventful struggle, the preacher feels called on solemnly to admonish the country against the " spirit of infidelity, selfishness, luxury, and dissatisfaction which so deeply marks our our present manners." [5]

Samuel Cooper, he who died in 1783, and who had previously preached in 1756, discoursed also in 1780 before John Hancock, the Senate, and House, " Being the day of the Commencement of the Constitution, and Inauguration of the New Government." This was, as appears, the day of general election under the new Constitution, so that here is a second instance of two Election Sermons in one year. It has been proposed, rather senselessly it seems, to count into the total the two extra sermons for 1775 and

---

[1] Webster's Election Sermon for 1777, p. 30.
[2] Payson's Election Sermon for 1778, p. 11.   [3] *Ibid.* p. 37, *note.*
[4] Stillman's Election Sermon for 1779, p. 8.
[5] Howard's Election Sermon for 1780, p. 47.

1780, in order to fill up the numerical gap of the years 1752 and 1764. Cooper's effort was a model of the patriotic sermon, and was full of that dignity which in some way we have associated with many of the sayings, writings, and actions of the nobler characters of our Revolutionary era. The preacher was then approaching mature age; his Artillery sermon had been delivered when he was but twenty-six years of age, and his first Election Sermon when he was thirty-one. This later sermon of 1780 had the distinction of being translated into Dutch, and was inserted in the *Verzameling van stukken tot de dertien Vereenigde Staeten van Noord-America betrekkelijk*" (Leyden, 1781).

Of the impassioned appeal to patriotism, well panoplied with italics, exclamation-points, and other weapons from the typographical armory, the sermon of Jonas Clark of Lexington for 1781 is a good specimen.

Not often did our ancestors venture away from the Scriptures to find elsewhere a quotation to grace diction. It is safe to say that Zabdiel Adams, in quoting "vanish like the baseless fabrick of a vision,"[1] was the first in this list of preachers to borrow from Shakespeare. He misquotes, to be sure, but the attempt was commendable. Several phrases used by this preacher are worth remembering; as when, for instance, urging continuation of the war, he exclaims: "It is better to be *free among the dead*, than slaves among the living."[2]

Moses Hemmenway of Wells, Maine, who preached in 1784, was a rather eccentric person, and this fact may possibly have caused the apparent anxiety on the part of the Legislature that he should decline his invitation to preach.[3]

No sooner was the Revolution well past than the "sins of the day" again began to be attacked with undiminished vigor. Joseph Lyman especially, in 1787, waxes very hot over popular vices.

---

[1] Adams's Election Sermon for 1782, p. 49.　　　[2] *Ibid*. p. 58.

[3] Resolve requesting the Governor and Council to appoint a gentleman to preach the election sermon, in case that Mr. *Hemmenway* declines. 25 *March*, 1784.

Whereas the great distance of the Rev. *Moses Hemmenway*, chosen by the House to preach upon the next annual election, has prevented his giving his answer, . . . Resolved: etc. (Resolves of the General Court, March, 1784, No. ccii., p. 151.)

His sermon likewise reviews at some length Shays's Rebellion, which had ended early in that year.

The declination of Joseph Lathrop to preach in 1793 is a matter of regret; for had he accepted, the one blot on the escutcheon of our Election Sermons had probably never been. As it happens, however, the only instance of dishonesty in connection with this custom is to be found in the sermon of Samuel Parker of Trinity Church, Boston, for that year. A large part of the matter of Parker's address was taken bodily and without acknowledgment from Jacques Saurin's " Harmony of Religion and Civil Polity," which may be found in the fourth volume of the edition of Saurin's Sermons in seven volumes.

The preachers at this period, in common with all New England, were throwing up their hands in horror at the excesses of the French Revolution, and were trying to stay its influence on this side of the ocean. As a matter of course, this anti-Gallic sentiment was that of strong Federalists, and came from such men as John Mellen, who preached in 1797, and who speaks of John Adams as "that highly respectable character." [1] It was Adams himself who referred to the Vice-Presidency as a " respectable situation." [2]

A Constant Reader wrote to the " New England Telegraph and Eclectic Review " in 1836 (II. 337–351), " It is long since Dr. Emmons's Election Sermon, preached at Boston in 1798, was out of print," and requested a reprint. Moses Thacher, the editor of this Review, accordingly printed the discourse entire.

The century was very young when Aaron Bancroft began the familiar cry, " O tempora!" He found more virtue in the early settlers, and among them greater purity in elections. That voting was honest is doubtless true, although in the Colony Records it may be seen that even in our golden era measures were taken against throwing an excess of beans as ballots. In 1803 Reuben Puffer predicts the downfall of the Republic, — an idea not previously advanced in these sermons, but yet the natural outcome of extravagant laudation of the past from the pulpit. In the next year, 1804, Samuel Kendal threw doubts on the doctrine of equality. In 1806 and 1808 the preachers are a little optimistic

---

[1] Mellen's Election Sermon for 1797, p. 32.
[2] Morse's "John Adams," p. 248.

in their views, — one of them, Thomas Allen, finding, even in the face of the embargo, that this country is "not the abode of wretchedness."[1] This preacher is also refreshingly brief.

It is hardly necessary to explain that most of the worthy gentlemen who had preached for some time were Federalists, and that from 1801 to 1806 their sermons were delivered in the audience of that unwavering partisan, Caleb Strong. They had the comforting assurance that their utterances were indorsed by the "respectability" of the State, and consequently out of the abundance of their hearts their mouths spake. But there is a limit even to the license tolerated in an Election Sermon, for although the custom began with some very free speech, it was terminated doubtless because of over-indulgence in the same privilege. David Osgood, in 1809, must have been peculiarly exasperating to Republican listeners, so much so perhaps that they were the more ready to take quick offence if due cause was given. The cause did arise when Elijah Parish of Byfield uttered words, at the election in 1810, full of that peculiar vehemence which such men as Timothy Pickering and his sympathizers so dearly loved. There was, however, nothing more violent in Parish's words than in parts of Osgood's address. Parish calls the government atheistical, and an ally of Napoleon, — Napoleon of course being the veritable Antichrist to a good Federalist. He continues: "The Chieftain of Europe, drunk with blood, casts a look upon us; he raises his voice, more terrible than the midnight yell of savages, at the doors of our forefathers."[2] So little was all this to the taste of the Legislature, that no majority was found to ask the plain-spoken minister for a copy of his sermon for the press; he accordingly was under the necessity, unique in the later annals of this subject, of printing at his own and his subscribers' expense. The pamphlet had the unusual honor of two editions. If one recalls the impressive lessons upon the duty of obedience to rulers, and then reads the vilifications of those in authority in the Election discourses of this period, the thoroughly bad temper of Massachusetts, exhibited just before and during the war of 1812, may be plainly understood. Here may be seen a reflection of the true spirit of the times, and that spirit History will decide was bad. Not all these sermons, however, which relate to

[1] Allen's Election Sermon for 1808. p. 13.
[2] Parish's Election Sermon for 1810, p. 21.

the events preceding and during the war of 1812 are of questionable patriotism. Edmund Foster in 1812 was on the side of the government and in favor of the war; but what can be said of James Flint's defence of England in 1815, or of his referring to the taking of Washington as "the attack of the enemy upon the immediate seat and citadel of improvidence and imbecility, the head-quarters of the redoubtable heroes of Bladensburg?"[1]

Among many excellent discourses, it has seemed to me that the one delivered by William Jenks in 1820 was exceptionally eloquent. This was the year of the formation of the new State of Maine, and the preacher was from Bath. The rather unusual fortune of two editions befell Daniel Sharp's sermon for 1824, perhaps by reason of his cheerful vaticinations for the future of the Nation. The tone of Moses Stuart's sermon for 1827 was thoroughly democratic; he was followed the next year, in an address of commendable brevity, by James Walker, who spoke again in 1863, forty-nine years after his graduation at Harvard. In 1830, Channing spoke on "Spiritual Freedom," — a theme congenial to him.

The simple and almost familiar discourse of Leonard Withington in 1831 is refreshing after much that was stately, not to say stilted. He speaks at some length of the former influence of the clergy; and of the Revolution he says frankly, "We lost more in our morals, in the single war of the Revolution, than we ever lost before."[2]

In 1832, when Paul Dean preached, an important change was made in the date of Election Day; whereas it was formerly the first Wednesday after Easter term, it was now appointed for the first Wednesday in January, and so continued thereafter.

Next to the "insidious wiles of foreign influence," of the Farewell Address, the two chief causes which, the Jeremiahs tell us, are finally to destroy this republic, are party spirit and the indifference of citizens to public affairs. "The Duties and Dangers of those who are born Free," by William B. O. Peabody in 1833, speaks as if these were common political shortcomings of that date.

After the democratic fervor in most of these sermons, Jonathan M. Wainwright's sermon for 1835, on the "Inequality of individual

---

[1] Flint's Election Sermon for 1815, p. 18.
[2] Withington's Election Sermon for 1831, p. 21.

wealth the ordinance of Providence and essential to civilization," must have been annoying to public taste. At this period there was much talk about a prevailing tendency towards communism; to what particular "craze" reference was had I do not know. That there was such a disturbance is evident from Wainwright's sermon, and likewise from that of Andrew Bigelow in 1836,—altogether a "respectable" discourse, and not at all like its great predecessors of the Revolutionary period. Bigelow preached before Samuel T. Armstrong, who was not only Acting Governor, but also at the same time Lieutenant-Governor and Mayor of Boston. His sermon contains a list of Election preachers; as also did David Osgood's in 1809.

Although preachers may have overestimated its effects, it is still true that party feeling was then running very high, — so high that many ministers felt it to be their duty to try to abate the political fever, rather than repeat the indiscreet zeal of the pulpit in the times of 1812. The remarks of a pious and thoughtful man like John Codman, in his sermon for 1840, are well worth reading.

Samuel C. Jackson was well known for his outspokenness, and by reason of it he almost shared the fate of Elijah Parish in 1810. His sermon for 1843 narrowly escaped the condemnation of the Senate. Dr. Park, in his "Memorial of Jackson," gives an account of this episode, and I shall repeat it: —

"He published a few terse essays for the newspapers and only four sermons. One of these sermons illustrates his characteristic style of preaching, not into the air, nor to the winds, but to the men and women before him. . . . Seldom, if ever, has an Election sermon produced a greater excitement. The first printed edition of it (three thousand copies) was soon exhausted, and a second edition soon published. Some of the newspapers printed copious extracts from it, and characterized it as 'vigorous,' 'bold,' 'eloquent,' 'masterly,' 'honest,' 'independent;' others condemned it. Eight of the senators opposed, and thirteen favored the Senate's vote of thanks to the preacher. On reading the sermon at the present day, one finds it difficult to imagine the reasons for such violence of opposition to it; but on comparing it with the political evils which were rife at the time of its delivery, one sees that it was a sermon for that particular time. . . ." [1]

[1] Memorial of Samuel C. Jackson, by Edwards A. Park, Andover, 1871, p. 18.

4

There is certainly an astonishing dearth of amenities in such a subject as this. Two hundred and more sermons are not a favorable field in which to turn up many nuggets of wit. The sermon of Milton Palmer Braman for 1845 is a grateful oasis in a vast desert of words. Although it contains eighty-five pages, it has within them a number of pleasantries, and is extremely optimistic. Braman speaks tartly of South Carolina executing "her alarming threat of withdrawing her protection from the general government, and shutting the United States out of the Union."[1] Of the then flourishing transcendental movement, he says, rather neatly, "Christianity needs Christianizing, and its spirit of love to be sublimated into the transcendental, super-exquisite, double-refined philanthropy of the apostles of a civilized Gospel."[2] He comments at some length on Know-Nothingism, which had not then come to be known by that name, and is opposed to immigration of the ignorant.

As late as 1848, it is curious that Alexander II. Vinton should insist on the divine origin of government, something which Election preachers, almost without exception, have been strenuous to deny, following, as I have said elsewhere, the theory of Locke.

The Rev. John Pierce, to whom lovers of antiquity, and of Election Sermons in particular, owe gratitude, preached in 1849. He was, I believe, the longest graduated, at the time of the delivery of his sermon, of any in the long list of preachers, having then been an alumnus of Harvard College for fifty-six years. He deals with the question of temperance, on which these sermons had long been silent ; and he also speaks of the charitable endeavors of Miss Dorothea L. Dix. At the end of his address is a list of Election Sermons, with notes which I have had occasion to use. Dr. Pierce had collected for himself thirteen sermons of the seventeenth century, all but four of the eighteenth, and of the nineteenth all down to 1849. This, the finest collection of the kind at that time, was bound by decades, when possible, and after the owner's death was sent to the Massachusetts Historical Society's Library.

It cannot escape notice that the sermon of the great logician of Andover, Edwards A. Park, for 1851, on the "Indebtedness of the State to the Clergy,"[3] evaded the most absorbing moral question

---

[1] Braman's Election Sermon for 1845, p. 34.   [2] Ibid. p. 40.
[3] Reprinted in Dr. Park's "Discourses on some Theological Doctrines as related to the Religious Character." (1885.)

then before mankind. Coming just after the advocacy of a theocratic democracy in the discourses of Alexander H. Vinton in 1848, and of Edward Hitchcock in 1850, the contrast is sharp which is presented by Rollin H. Neale's statement in 1852 that government, "in its corporate capacity, has no more to do with religion than the directors of a bank or the superintendents of a railway." [1] This preacher was not a sympathizer with Know-Nothingism. He has besides a long note on the now almost forgotten mission of Kossuth.

Not much longer could the discussion of what was uppermost in the popular mind be scorned or avoided. Even the Election preacher must utter something besides graceful periods, and at last even the Vicar of Bray must become a partisan. In the midst of the clamor for human rights could be heard at times the small voice of the conservative pulpit. He who spoke in 1855 carefully avoids all discussion of anything of the slightest contemporary interest or importance, but has his fling at "a self-righteous, self-seeking philanthrophy," [2] by which he would seem to mean the anti-slavery agitation.

It is impossible now to discover how many copies of the earlier sermons were printed in an edition; but at about this time, in the order to print, the number is specified. A few of the sermons were printed as follows: in 1855, 3,000 copies; in 1856, 4,000; in 1857, 3,000; in 1858, 4,000; in 1859, 2,000; in 1860, 3,000; in 1861 and 1863, 8,000; in 1864, 5,000; in 1872, 4,000; in 1873, 3,000; in 1874, 3,000; and in 1876, 1,000 only.

Although the authors of many of these sermons failed to perceive the inevitable drift of public affairs, yet it is creditable to them that so few had "notions" to advance. I have met, in the course of my ramblings through these pages, no proposition more singular than that advanced by Raymond H. Seeley, in 1856, to obviate the evils of spoils-hunting. He would have "put up, annually, certain sums of money and badges of distinctions — stars, garters, and crosses of the legion of honor — to be won by the ballot-box, and distributed among those parties who should secure the largest number of votes." [3]

---

[1] Neale's Election Sermon for 1852, p. 27, note.
[2] Samuel Kirkland Lothrop's Election Sermon for 1855, p. 14.
[3] Seeley's Election Sermon for 1856, p. 23.

Governor Henry J. Gardner was the successful candidate of the Know-Nothing party from 1855 to 1858. In his audience were spoken many things supposed to be grateful to the sentiments of the select political organization which elected him. No other Election Sermon that I can recall is so violent in its religious and race prejudice as John Pike's long diatribe in 1857 against Roman Catholicism. We must forgive this preacher his rashness, for he tells the story (perhaps unconscious of its merits) of the toasting of Archbishop Hughes at Blackwell's Island, New York, as "Our illustrious guest, the representative of the large majority of the inhabitants of the Island!"[1]

Taken as a whole, how few the useful and practical suggestions for every-day life in this immense array of discourses! But as the list grows longer there is noticeably less of the merely doctrinal and conventional, and more, very much more, of effective Christianity and humanity. Edward Everett Hale's address in 1859 was eminently useful. Though very close to the eve of war, it does not refer to national affairs, but is directed against red tape, dead letter, and other evils of bureaucracy, particularly as they relate to public charities. He makes the interesting statement that three times as many men were imprisoned in 1857 as in 1844.[2]

"It would be folly," said Austin Phelps in 1861, "to predict the intelligence of to-morrow's telegraph;"[3] and in his tribute to Freedom he refers significantly to the "hush which precedes the earthquake."[4] The earth had quaked effectually before the next Election Day came, on which occasion William R. Alger spoke. The generation which was young when the Civil War began cannot easily comprehend the spirit of this preacher's address, which seems to refer to some peculiar phase of the public mind. To him the eager patriotism of the time appeared "more like the pride of the country leaping up to avenge an insult."[5] James Walker in his sermon for 1863, yearns for another Washington, while by contrast, the next year, William A. Stearns rejoices that "there is a power in the land hardly second to that of an immense army,"[6]

---

[1] Pike's Election Sermon for 1857, p. 31.
[2] Hale's Election Sermon for 1859, p. 23.
[3] Phelps's Election Sermon for 1861, p. 56.   [4] Ibid. p. 48.
[5] Alger's Election Sermon for 1862, p. 40.
[6] Stearns's Election Sermon for 1864, p. 38.

meaning by this the personal character of Abraham Lincoln. "Thank God," he begins, "we have still a country!" During the delivery of his sermon, Dr. Stearns had the misfortune to drop his manuscript. It is remembered of the incident that he asked Dr. Blagden to pray during the picking up of the widely scattered pages.

"Oh! that New England might be, late and forever, what she was at first — Puritan!" [1] — is the solemn wish of Andrew L. Stone in 1865. His words are full of kindness for the desolate South, and for the future of the African race; but he inveighs against "that foul monster, fouler and more misshapen than Satan saw sitting portress at the gate of hell — PARTY SPIRIT." [2] Mr. Grinnell, speaking in 1871, takes a different view when he says: "Rather than an indifferentist, give me a violent partisan; rather than a conservative bigot, give me a radical fanatic." [3]

For eloquence pure and simple, Alonzo H. Quint's patriotic discourse in 1866 has struck me as most noteworthy. It is one long, breathless sentence on the power of a democracy to carry on a war in a loyal spirit. In this pamphlet was a list of Election preachers.

In 1868, Dr. James Freeman Clarke comes back to the Gospel of Practical Reform, which the necessities of war had stopped since Mr. Hale had proclaimed it in 1859. He dwells on prison reform, makes the first important defence in these sermons of women's rights, and throws his influence against corporal punishment in schools. How a Stoughton or a Torrey would have shuddered at so practical and direct a view of things. No Hebrew, no Greek, not even a bit of Latin, to garnish the straightforward and simple English! Dr. Clarke found the next year a direct opponent of his views in Benjamin F. Clark, who held that the object of law is to protect, not to reform. At the close of the sermon a hymn seems to have been sung, which, so far as I have noticed, is the only hymn printed in connection with an Election Sermon.

In Grinnell's sermon on Fanaticism in 1871, Mr. Henry H. Edes published his full and important list of Election preachers, upon which I have much relied.

Owing to the declination by William H. H. Murray of an invitation to preach in 1872, Andrew P. Peabody accepted the honor, and

---

[1] Stone's Election Sermon for 1865, p. 16.   [2] *Ibid.* p. 30.
[3] Grinnell's Election Sermon for 1871, p. 26.

discoursed on "The Rights and Dangers of Property." It will be remembered that this was a time of great dissatisfaction in national affairs. The preacher seems to have fallen into the critical vein, and takes a censorious view, even going so far as to say that "We are probably the most heavily taxed people upon the face of the earth." [1] Dr. Peabody's sermon was widely read.

In 1875, Edwin C. Bolles of Salem preached, but his sermon was not printed. There is tolerable certainty that several sermons which were delivered were never printed, particularly those for 1713 and 1717; but it is positive that the sermon for 1875 was never given to the press, although its publication was requested. It is unfortunate that to Mr. Bolles should attach the distinction of being the first preacher to break a clean record of sermons printed continuously since 1765. He seems, however, to have had a reasonable excuse, and I shall not hesitate to give it. It appears that the business of assembling the legislators and of choosing officers had for some years past taken so much of the attention of the General Court, that by the time it was ready to hear the Sermon the hour was quite late, and many of the members failed to attend the ceremony. The preacher was not infrequently detained some time before all was in readiness. This was especially the case in 1875. The Court was late, the audience was so small as to fill about one quarter of the seats, the eloquent preacher was kept waiting. He finally delivered an able discourse, and was, as a matter of course, asked to prepare a copy for the press; but the copy was never presented, and so the long chain was at last broken.

As a result of this culmination of recent delays and inconveniences attending the ceremony, a resolve was approved on 12 May, 1875, "That the annual election sermon shall hereafter be preached in some house of religious worship in the city of Boston, to be designated each year by the Governor, under whose general direction proper arrangements for the service shall be made." [2]

The last few sermons have a peculiar, even melancholy, interest. James L. Hill's for 1878 is unlike the rest in being full of footnotes; Alexander McKenzie's for 1879 was full of poetical quotations; while in 1880 Daniel W. Waldron's tells an "affecting anec-

---

[1] Peabody's Election Sermon for 1872, p. 19.
[2] Resolves of 1875, chap. 62.

dote," — the first of the homiletic sort which I recall.[1] The most elegantly and attractively printed sermon was Daniel L. Furber's in 1881. It had the honor of two editions, and contains some interesting historical data concerning its predecessors.

There may be some who are of the opinion that this custom fell into disfavor through lack of ability or interest on the part of the ministry of later years. Let such read the sermon for 1882, by Joseph F. Lovering of Worcester, "The Shields of the Earth belong to the Lord." The request to print calls it an "instructive, patriotic, and valuable discourse," and so it is; not one of this long array is more so. Compare its humanity and enthusiasm with the dry, dull pedantry of so much of the remote past of this sort of literature. In 1883, Robert R. Meredith dwelt on the observance of Sunday, marriage laws, intemperance, and other practical questions.

For a few of the later years the sermons were delivered in King's Chapel. It was destined that the last ever spoken should depart from this precedent, since the ceremonies for 1884 took place in the Columbus Avenue Universalist Church. The pastor, the Rev. Alonzo A. Miner, chose for his subject, "The Rectitude of Government the Source of its Power." After a vigorous attack upon social and political evils, among which he included some alleged evils which were dwelt upon in a way which was perhaps intended to be offensive to many of his hearers, he wound up with a salutation to the out-going governor, General Benjamin F. Butler, who had been the chief magistrate during 1883, and had just been defeated for re-election. "Your great success through a long professional career, achieved by extraordinary ability and rare personal energy, command in this hour of retirement from the gubernatorial office general recognition."[2] The hot blood of party strife had not sufficiently cooled from a campaign of almost unparalleled intensity to tolerate this, and shortly afterwards the Election Sermon was abolished. The motion to abolish the custom was made by the Hon. John F. Andrew, son of Governor John A. Andrew. The direct causes were very likely political opposition, and a dislike to hear moral questions discussed politically by ministers; but deeper than the spleen of legislators was the fact that

---

[1] Waldron's Election Sermon for 1880, p. 20.
[2] Miner's Election Sermon for 1884, p. 46.

the religious character of the people of this Commonwealth no longer appeared to demand a continuance of the old custom.

It is a curious coincidence, though two hundred and fifty years separated the times of their delivery, that the first and the last Massachusetts Election Sermons both ran counter to public sentiment. Cotton's interference in politics in 1634 met with a significant rebuke from his listeners; and in 1884 Dr. Miner hastened an end which, regret it as we may, we can hardly call untimely.

In reading many pages of so much that is representative of New England thought, and of that thought often at its best, two objects have been uppermost, — one, to discover the opinions of our ministry during this stretch of years concerning the sin of slavery; the other, to get facts concerning public morals, especially in relation to intemperance.

To acquit the clergy of New England of indifference in their attitude toward the "sum of all villanies" would be most agreeable if it were possible. The evidence does not stand in our favor; and a candid search only enables one to add more black marks to the unfavorable record compiled by the late Dr. George H. Moore.

The lack of moral enthusiasm on this topic appears in a worse light because, so far as we can learn, great freedom of speech was tolerated on this occasion, even just before the Revolution, when the sermons, being circulated as political and social tracts, were expressly adapted as means to promote reform. It was not as if the ministers had to invent the moral conception that slave-trading or slave-holding was iniquitous; the Body of Liberties early had in some way recognized this fact.[1] Good men, too, made their protests. John Eliot, in 1675, remonstrated against selling Indians into slavery. Cotton Mather's sentiments in this matter were humane. In 1700 Samuel Sewall published his "The Selling of Joseph," — "the first public plea for the emancipation of the negro;"[2] and later Woolman's voice, which was raised against

---

[1] See Article 91, "Body of Liberties," in 3 Massachusetts Historical Collections, vii. 231. I do not forget that Dr. Moore, speaking of a case of slave-trading on a Boston vessel in 1645, says: "In all the proceedings of the General Court on this occasion, there is not a trace of anti-slavery opinion or sentiment." — *Notes on the History of Slavery in Massachusetts*, p. 30.

[2] See Mr. Goodell's communication on John Saffin and his slave Adam at the March, 1893, Meeting of this Society, *ante*, p. 85 *et seq.*

the enormity, was heard in New England. It may easily have happened that some earlier mention in this series of sermons has escaped my notice; but I do not recall anything of importance antedating Cooke's discourse for 1770, in which he eloquently says: "I trust, on this occasion, I may, without offence, plead the cause of our African slaves; and humbly propose the pursuit of some effectual measure, at least, to prevent the further importation of them." [1] The pulpit of Election Day had then been silent on this theme almost one hundred and forty years.

It is well understood that, in the midst of the Revolution, William Gordon was dismissed from the chaplaincy of the General Court because of his views on slavery.[2] Free speech proved as disastrous to the preacher in 1778 as it did in 1634 and 1884. Yet in 1779 not only anti-slavery but emancipation was advocated by Samuel Stillman: "May the year of jubilee soon arrive, when Africa shall cast the look of gratitude to these happy regions, for the TOTAL EMANCIPATION of HER SONS!" [3] Moses Hemmenway, in 1784, boldly declares that "That inhuman monster SLAVERY, which has too long been tolerated, is at length proscribed. . . . And it is devoutly wished that the turf may lie firm upon its grave." [4] After this is a moral interregnum until 1805, when John Allyn takes up the subject, to drop it speedily "lest something unwelcome should obtrude itself in regard to the social condition of some of our sister States." [5] Three decades more of Election Sermons and Daniel Dana in 1837 speaks out a little more boldly. He would not disturb the political side of the problem, but would attack its weak position on the moral side. Dana also devotes a few words to the Indian policy. Andrew Bigelow in 1836, and David Damon in 1841, in extremely conservative sermons, were unfriendly to the anti-slavery spirit. That, however, was already a spirit which could not be laid by hostile words. There is no uncertainty in the boldness of George Putnam's anti-slavery sentiments in 1846, nor does he omit to express himself on the coming Mexican war. The clergy were

---

[1] Cooke's Election Sermon for 1770, p. 41.
[2] George H. Moore's Notes on the History of Slavery in Massachusetts, p. 194.
[3] Stillman's Election Sermon for 1779. p. 35.
[4] Hemmenway's Election Sermon for 1784. p. 37.
[5] Allyn's Election Sermon for 1805, p. 25.

at last gaining moral courage. The habitual caution of age was moved to express itself when the venerable Dr. Pierce in 1849 assured his hearers that "we shall try by all feasible means to be rid of slavery." [1]

To those who believed in what was then called the Higher Law, Dr. Neale's sermon for 1852 was a wet-blanket; but the next year Samuel Wolcott, in the longest discussion yet devoted to this subject, made amends for previous lukewarmness. "Disobedience is a solemn duty," he affirms, of the Fugitive Slave Law. In 1860, at the eleventh hour, Thomas D. Anderson shows that lack of sympathy with the popular sentiment common to so many of the clergy, when he says, "The exchange of slavery for bloodshed, of civilized homes for servile elevation, the gain of the form of equality, at the dictation of despotic force, makes no progress." [2]   With a very few exceptions, therefore, I am convinced that the preachers of the Massachusetts Election Sermons were not outspoken as to slavery. It will have to be admitted that there were two sides to the slavery question, else it would not have been a question. It must also be conceded that the General Court was slow in inviting preachers of a radical turn of mind to address it, and hence it was that men like Lyman Beecher, Theodore Parker, and James Freeman Clarke, were ignored in the critical days before the Civil War.

But there were other evils nearer home which no ministry of any age may treat lightly. Chief among these evils was intemperance. The fact of slavery was patent to everybody, but I cannot find that the fact of drunkenness was equally plain to the ethical perception of our preachers.

The fight against New England's greatest social enemy began early; and yet *ab initio* there were those who could see nothing but an almost Utopian condition of things. The stern witch judge, in 1668, bitterly cries out against "Revellings and Drunkenness;" on the other hand, however, Hutchinson quotes a letter written in 1660 in which the writer states that he "had lived several years in the country and never saw a person drunk nor never heard a profane oath." [3]   Hutchinson states elsewhere that he

---

[1] Pierce's Election Sermon for 1849, p. 48.

[2] Anderson's Election Sermon for 1860, p. 26.

[3] History of Massachusetts, i. 443. I think that Hutchinson is here trying to quote Giles Firmin, whose very words are given later.

"never heard of a separation, under the first charter, *a mensa et thoro.*"[1] Stoughton was not the only pessimist in this respect. Willard, in 1682, speaks of "beastly drunkenness;" and in 1689, Cotton Mather, who had a modern zeal for temperance reform, mildly asks, " Whether the *Multitude* or *Quality* of *Drinking-Houses,* in the midst of us, had not once been a *Stumbling-block of our Iniquity.*"[2] The next year he is covertly censuring men of the Andros stamp who, he thought, tended to spoil the simple morals of New Englanders, "and learn them to Drink and Drab, and Game, and profane the Sabbath, and *Sin against the Hope of their Fathers.*"[3]

Joseph Belcher, in 1701, speaks of the sins of sensuality, idleness, and of drunkenness, especially among the "miserable Indians;" Estabrook, in 1705, continues in the same strain. In 1708, John Norton (of Hingham) arraigns a black host, — "Atheism, prophaneness, sensuality, pride, oppression, lukewarmness," etc.;[4] but drunkenness is not among them. " Is not our Land deluged with *Intemperance* and *Drunkness ?* "[5] asks Ebenezer Pemberton in 1710; and later on he speaks of "*Frauds* and *Forgeries* committed upon our *Bills of Publick Credit.*"[6] The year before, Grindall Rawson inquires: "Doth not the Shameful and worse than Bruitish Sin of Drunkenness, like an irresistible Inundation, threaten to carry all before it?"[7] and, further, "Are not *hainous,* and fearful breaches of the Seventh Commandment . . . become exceeding frequent?"[8] Peter Thacher is more specific in his charges: "What excessive Tipling and Drinking, which like a Flood even drowns much of Christianity in several places? Especially on Training-day-evenings, which things ought not to be."[9] A few years later, William Williams of Hatfield discourses against disrespect to rulers, laxity as to church-going, and drunkenness. Of the last he says: "It is almost incredible what is said of the Quantities of Rhum bro't into the Country. . . . In many places the *Minister* has but few Visitors to enquire the way of Life: but the *Inn-keeper* is throng'd with

[1] Hutchinson's History of Massachusetts, i. 445.
[2] Mather's Election Sermon for 1689, p. 26.
[3] Mather's Election Sermon for 1690, p. 31.
[4] Norton's Election Sermon for 1708, p. 15.
[5] Pemberton's Election Sermon for 1710, p. 99.   [6] *Ibid.* p. 101.
[7] Rawson's Election Sermon for 1709, p. 35.   [8] *Ibid.* p. 35.
[9] Thacher's Election Sermon for 1711, p. 29.

company. . . . When they come from Work they go to the *Tavern ;* when dismissed from Trainings they go to the *Tavern.*" [1]

It has seemed to me a reasonable theory that, during the political quiet in New England of the first half of the eighteenth century, an opportunity may have been afforded to the ministry for inquiring more fully into the moral condition of the country. There were no more witches to try, and the Indians were under control; there was really nothing to ponder but the debased currency, the duty to rulers, and man's unceasing weakness and folly. Some ministers endeavored seriously to work a reform, and did not content themselves with conventional regrets over wickedness. "Let it be seriously considered," said Joseph Baxter, in 1727, "whether the Multiplying of Houses that are Licensed to Sell Strong Drink be not the occasion of a great deal of Sin. And is there no remedying of that? Is there nothing more to be done to keep Town-Dwellers from Sotting away their Time at Taverns? And cannot there be something done that will be more effectual to prevent the making of Indians Drunk?" [2]

Thomas Prince, in his sermon for 1730, makes a statement which must have astonished even the generally blameless New Englanders of those days, when he said, "I never heard a *Profane Oath or Curse* till I was *Fifteen* Years of Age, when I came down and heard them first from a Profane Youth of our Metropolis." [3] Still more astounding is the assertion that "Profane Swearers and Drunkards are not known in the Land." [4] If this refers, as must be its intention, to the pristine days of the Colony, Winthrop's Journal conclusively disproves the existence of such felicitous conditions.

Giles Firmin is commonly supposed to have declared in a sermon [5] before the Houses of Lords and Commons, with the Assembly of Divines, at Westminster, that "he never saw a Beggar, nor a Man overcome with strong Drink, nor did he ever hear a profane Oath among them." Israel Loring, who quotes Giles Firmin, as above, in

[1] Williams's Election Sermon for 1719, p. 25.
[2] Baxter's Election Sermon for 1727, p. 32.
[3] Prince's Election Sermon for 1730, p. 35.
[4] *Ibid.* p. 29.
[5] John Ward Dean, in his Brief Memoir of Firmin (p. 11) quotes this a little differently, and seems inclined to doubt if the utterance was that of Firmin.

his Sermon for 1737,[1] proposed that "No Person be allowed to sell strong Drink, but what are of approved Sobriety and good Conversation, Men of Honesty, and good Order."[2] A strong voice against this "Sin, which threatens to Ruin this Land,"[3] was raised by Daniel Lewis in 1748. From that time on, for a hundred years, the Election pulpit was virtually silent on this topic. It was not, I think, until Dr. Pierce's sermon in 1849 that the subject was again taken up in earnest.

What is now understood as Prohibition was favored in 1854 by Miner Raymond, and for the first time in these sermons. After him there was a gap, until Henry W. Warren, in 1867, once more revived the theme, which at last, however timidly it has usually been handled, was thoroughly and finally discussed by Dr. Miner.

Not only were the early preachers alive to moral delinquencies, but they were watchful over the wants of education. The first sermons contain many urgent demands for enforcement of laws regarding the "inferior schools." Prince, in 1730, speaking of advantages in his day, mentions "*Grammar Schools* in every Town of an hundred Families, free for the Poorest without Expence."[4]

The custom of preaching the Election Sermon was early felt by the preachers themselves to be important and worthy of maintenance. But Bishop (then the Reverend Mr.) Huntington, in 1858, seems to have anticipated its doom: "If it ever sinks into a mere routine, — the ghastly effigy of a departed sincerity, — it will be because some generation has not honesty and courage to drop the form with the life."[5] The true object of preserving the custom would seem to have been best expressed by the preacher for 1874, when he calls the Election ceremony "a service whose value is not so much in the words that may be spoken, as in the reverent act that is publicly done."[6] But pious wish of preacher, and sentiment for a venerable and peculiar New-England institution cherished in the hearts of a few lovers of the past, could not save the Election Sermon. It seems to have been abolished in a Legislative huff,

---

[1] Loring's Election Sermon for 1737, p. 27.   [2] *Ibid.* p. 51.

[3] Lewis's Election Sermon for 1748, p. 17.

[4] Prince's Election Sermon for 1730, p. 34.

[5] Huntington's Election Sermon for 1858, p. 8.

[6] Richard Gleason Greene's Election Sermon for 1874, p. 24.

but in reality the legislators were tired of it, and the people were forgetting that there was such a thing.

Elections were generally held in May,[1] the last Wednesday in Easter term, until 1832, when the time was changed to the first Wednesday in January. The severities of a New-England winter, and the still greater severities of a New-England spring, would not at first have allowed an earlier gathering of the representative free-men. As it was, the arrangements for their reception were meagre, and their place of gathering rude. We do not learn that any meeting-house was erected until 1632, in which year there was built a one-story thatched-roof structure in what is now State Street, on the site of Brazer's Building.[2] Afterwards the ser-vices were held in the new meeting-house, which was built in 1640, on the site of the Rogers Building on Washington Street nearly opposite the head of State Street. Lechford says, "the generall and great quarter Courts are kept" here.[3] Boston had then a fair-sized population, although the polls were meagre in number. Even as late as 1665 only ninety votes were thrown to elect deputies. The next place where the Sermon was preached was the Town House, which was given by Captain Keayne. This structure was finished about the year 1638. In 1711 it was burnt.[4] In 1713 the Council met in the new Town House, now the Old State House. During most of the time, however, the sermons were delivered in the Old South Church. After its disuse as a meeting-house, several were preached in King's Chapel, Hollis Street Church, and the new Old South Meeting-house; the last service, as has been said, was in the Columbus Avenue Universalist Church.

Until recent years considerable interest was shown not only in the ceremonies incident to Election day, but in the "spoken word" itself. We find several references to a "vast assembly;" and as far back as 1673 Oakes speaks of "this great Assembly (so con-

---

[1] By the Charter of 1691 the last Wednesday of May was established "Elec-tion-day," and a little later the Artillery election-day was established. — *Memo-rial History of Boston*, ii. 217.

[2] Memorial History of Boston, i. 119, *note*.

[3] Lechford's "Plain Dealing" (Trumbull's edition), p. 61.

[4] "And that desolating FIRE in our Metropolis, laying so much of our Glory in Ashes, destroying so many goodly Edifices, turning us out of doors, where these Solemnities have been so many years formerly Celebrated." — *Cheever's Election Sermon*, 1712, p. 11.

siderable as to the quality and publick capacity, as well as numerousness of the Auditors)." [1] There was, too, at times a listlessness which is sometimes observable at occasions of a public and official character. This inference may at least be drawn from Stillman's sermon in 1779, in the course of which he almost snappishly remarks: " Had this sentence been duly attended to at the time the sermon was delivered." [2]

In the last century, the legislators, rather than be deprived of a sermon, used sometimes to attend the regular Thursday, or Fifth-day, Lectures, — a series almost as ancient as the Election Sermons, and discontinued in 1833. [3] The Thursday Lecture thus attended would then be considered as an Election Sermon. Cases of this kind are John Webb's sermon, 11 February, 1780–81, and Thomas Foxcroft's, 23 November, 1727. [4]

In addition to the Election Sermon, the Artillery Election Sermon, which is still preached, and the Thursday Lecture, there was the Convention Sermon, — an interesting custom which is now observed, and which took its rise in the ceremonies of Election-day. The Rev. Alexander McKenzie has explained the origin of the Convention Sermon, which seems to have some connection with the present subject. [5]

The preaching of Election Sermons was not confined to Massachusetts, though, as the Rev. Albert Barnes remarks, " The custom, so far as we know, is peculiar to New England."

While the Plymouth Colony maintained a distinct government, Election Sermons were delivered there ; but I will not now attempt to describe them.

In Connecticut the Sermons were preached during a period of one hundred and fifty-six years, beginning in 1674 and ending in

---

[1] Oakes's Election Sermon for 1673, p. 21.

[2] Stillman's Election Sermon for 1779, p. 20, *note.*

[3] See Nathaniel L. Frothingham's " The Shade of the Past," Boston, 1833.

[4] In connection with these *extra* sermons, Dr. George H. Moore has called attention to the fact that there were generally two or more sessions, but not more than eight instances during the whole Provincial period of a second Assembly in one political year.

[5] Memorial History of Boston, ii. 223.

1830. In Chauncey Lee's Connecticut Election Sermon for 1813 an account of this extensive series may be found.[1]

The first Election Sermon in New Hampshire was delivered by Samuel McClintock in 1784; the last one was by Nathan Lord in 1831. No sermons were preached in 1793 or 1795.[2]

In 1778 the custom was begun in Vermont by Peter Bowers. There were no sermons for 1790, 1800, and 1831; but in 1834 Warren Skinner preached the last regular Vermont Election Sermon. In 1856 an attempt was made to revive the custom, which continued for three years, from 1856 to 1858.[3]

No set of the Massachusetts Sermons exists which can be called complete, — that is, which contains all those known to have been published. The best collection is in the Library of the Massachusetts Historical Society. It contains all but two, — those for 1696 and 1699. Of these Dr. Samuel A. Green, the Librarian of the Society, owns a copy of the sermon for 1699, by Increase Mather. Of the other, that for 1696, a copy is in possession of the American Antiquarian Society at Worcester, and another in the Boston Public Library. The Historical Society began early to strengthen itself in this important branch of the literature of the State, for in 1809 it was proposed "that Dr. Eliot, Mr. Alden, and Mr. McKean be a committee to prepare lists of preachers on the General Election, Artillery Election, and Convention, marking such of the sermons as the Society possess, which they shall endeavor to have inserted as appendices to the next sermons on those occasions."[4] In 1794 only twenty-one of those who preached before 1700 were known, and it was then thought that there was no sermon in 1721 on account of small-pox.

To the assiduity of Dr. John Pierce is due the best part of the

---

[1] A complete list, compiled by Ralph D. Smyth, is in the New England Historical and Genealogical Register for April, 1892, xlvi. 123.

[2] A complete list of the New-Hampshire Election Sermons is in the Congregational Quarterly for July, 1868, x. 240; and an earlier list is in William Allen's Sermon for 1818.

[3] An account of the Vermont discourses is in the Historical Magazine for March, 1868 (New Series, iii. 175). An earlier account, in the Congregational Quarterly for April, 1867 (ix. 187), was reprinted from the Vermont Record. Both articles are signed P. H. W., the initials, doubtless, of Pliny H. White.

[4] Massachusetts Historical Society's Proceedings, for May, 1809, i. 213.

Society's collection. In September, 1844, he stated that it had "been the aim of the subscriber from an early period of his ministry, to collect the printed Sermons delivered at the General Election of Massachusetts, which as fast as procured, are bound in decades." [1]

The next best set of the Election Sermons is in the Boston Public Library, if the volumes in the Old South, or Prince, Library be considered as part of the collections of that institution. This set contains all printed sermons, with the exception of the years 1671, 1695, 1700, 1708, 1711, 1715.

A complete set from 1747, with sixteen separate sermons previous to that date, is in the New York State Library. The Library of the Essex Institute has the sermons for the years 1683, 1698, 1703-1707, 1710, 1718, 1721, 1724-32, 1743-1884. The Andover Theological Seminary has the sermons from 1745, with about half a dozen exceptions. Other large libraries are so well represented that it is plain that this branch of Americana does not suffer neglect. Several private collectors have been industrious and successful. Dr. Pierce was the first and most fortunate. The late George Brinley had a finely preserved set running from the year 1793 to 1850, which is now in the Boston Public Library.

To be invited to preach was always an honor; several preachers were asked on more than one occasion. Thomas Shepard (the first), Jonathan Mitchel, Thomas Cobbett, Samuel Willard, Joshua Moody, Benjamin Colman, Samuel Cooper, and James Walker, each preached twice; Richard Mather, John Norton, and Samuel Torrey, each three times; Increase and Cotton Mather, each four times. Some of the earliest preachers may have officiated oftener. The three Mathers preached over four per cent of the whole two hundred and fifty-six sermons. It may be interesting to notice that Election Preachers were long lived. John Pierce was the longest graduated at the time of his preaching, — that is, fifty-six years; Samuel Cheever was also a graduate of fifty-six years, and James Walker of forty-nine years. Eighteen had been out of college for forty years or more when they preached.

It may be observed that Jonathan Mitchel, Cotton Mather, Joseph Belcher, and William Allen preached eleven years after

---

[1] Massachusetts Historical Society's Proceedings, ii. 293. 294.

graduation; Jonathan Mayhew, William B. Sprague, and John
W. Yeomans, ten years after; Charles E. Grinnell, nine years
after; and James L. Hill, seven years after. Dr. Pierce gives
twenty-eight and one half years as the average time of delivery
after graduation down to the year 1849.

From 1634 to 1879 one hundred and forty-three of the preachers
were Harvard graduates; there being one period, between 1681
and 1786, when only alumni of that college received the honor.
There were eight graduates of Cambridge University; five of Oxford; eleven of Yale; nine of Dartmouth College; four of Williams;
three of Amherst; two each of Bowdoin, Brown University, and
the University of Pennsylvania; one each of Columbia, Iowa, Miami,
Middlebury, Trinity, Union, University of New York, and Wesleyan. Of non-graduates there were only twenty, and of these,
fourteen were in the present century.

Five of the preachers went to college but did not graduate,
namely: Richard Mather, Thomas Cobbett, and John Oxenbridge,
to Oxford; Samuel Torrey and William Brimsmead, to Harvard.

In regard to the various denominations to which the preachers
belonged, Dr. Pierce gives statistics; but inasmuch as he put down
all Trinitarians and Unitarians as Congregationalists, I have not
made use of his results.

No Roman Catholic clergyman seems to have taken part in the
ceremonies of Election-day; it is worthy of note, however, that in
1791 Bishop John Carroll returned thanks at the Artillery Election dinner.[1]

Lists of Election Preachers were printed as follows: in Samuel
Deane's sermon for 1794, giving full name, residence, and text; in
David Osgood's for 1809, and in Andrew Bigelow's for 1836, both
giving full name, place, text, and size; in John Pierce's for 1849,
and in Alonzo H. Quint's for 1866, both giving full name, place,
text, Alma Mater, and date of graduation. The fullest as well as
latest list of the preachers of these Sermons, however, giving year,
full name, residence, text, Alma Mater, and date of graduation,
was compiled by Mr. Henry H. Edes, and published in an appendix
to Mr. Grinnell's Sermon. This list ends in 1871. The following
list prepared upon the same plan, completes the series: —

[1] American Museum, June, 1791, ix. App. iii. p. 43.

YEAR.	PREACHER.	RESIDENCE.	TEXT.	ALMA MATER.
1872	Andrew Preston Peabody	Cambridge.	Exodus xx. 15.	Harvard Coll. 1826.
1873	George Claude Lorimer [1].	Boston.	Matt. v. 17, 18.	
1874	Richard Gleason Greene [2].	Springfield.	Jeremiah ii. 31.	
1875	Edwin Cortland Bolles [3].	Salem.	Luke vi. 47, 48.	Trinity Coll. 1855.
1876	Samuel Wesley Foljambe [4]	Malden.	1 Kings viii. 57.	
1877	Benj. Franklin Hamilton.	Roxbury.	Rom. xiii. 1, 6.	Amherst Coll. 1861.
1878	James Langdon Hill . .	Lynn.	John iv. 38.	Iowa Coll. 1871.
1879	Alexander McKenzie . .	Cambridge.	James iv. 12.	Harvard Coll. 1859.
1880	Daniel Wingate Waldron	Boston.	Deut. viii. 2.	Bowdoin Coll. 1862.
1881	Daniel Little Furber . .	Newton.	Prov. xxix. 18.	Dartmouth Coll. 1843.
1882	Joseph Foster Lovering [5].	Worcester.	Ps. xlvii. 9.	
1883	Robert Rhoden Meredith [6]	Boston.	Prov. xiv. 34.	
1884	Alonzo Ames Miner [7]. .	Boston.	Ps. lxxxix. 14.	

[1] GEORGE CLAUDE LORIMER, born in Edinburgh, Scotland, 1838, took a course of study in Georgetown College, Ky., which gave him the degree of LL.D., in 1885; he has also received the degree of D.D. from Bethel College.

[2] RICHARD GLEASON GREENE, a graduate at Andover Theological Seminary, 1853; received the degree of A.M. from Yale, 1873.

[3] EDWIN CORTLAND BOLLES. The middle name of Mr. Bolles is variously given as Cortlandt and Courtland. I follow the spelling found in the Quinquennial Catalogue of Trinity College, Hartford, Conn.

[4] SAMUEL WESLEY FOLJAMBE, born in Leeds, England, received a liberal education; was first a Methodist, afterwards a Baptist, preacher. Received the degree of A.M. from Grandville College, Columbus, Ohio, and of D.D. from Central University, Pella, Iowa.

[5] JOSEPH FOSTER LOVERING, born in Kingston, Mass., 18 Aug. 1835; was in the Harvard College class of 1856, but did not graduate; and spent one year in the Divinity School at Cambridge. He was subsequently at Meadville, Pa.

[6] ROBERT RHODEN MEREDITH, born in Ireland, 1838, received the degree of A.M. from Wesleyan, 1875; and of D.D. from Dartmouth, 1882.

[7] ALONZO AMES MINER, President of Tufts College, 1862-1875; received the degree of A.M. from Tufts, 1861; of S.T.D., from Harvard, 1863; and of LL.D. from Tufts, 1875.

It would perhaps have been a gain to this paper to have tabulated many isolated bibliographical data; in fact it would have been agreeable to my plan to give a complete bibliography of the sermons, — if not of the entire series, at least of those delivered in the seventeenth century. Such expansion, however, has not seemed advisable in view of the fact that Dr. Samuel A. Green gives full and accurate titles of the earlier sermons in his recent and valuable List of Early American Imprints belonging to the Library of the Massachusetts Historical Society.[1]

Mr. Edes's list still remains, after nearly twenty-five years, a sound and useful piece of work. My supplementary list for 1872 to 1884 inclusive, and the following tabulations for years in which no sermons were preached, and for years in which sermons were preached and not printed, will, I trust, furnish all that is essential

[1] This List appeared while Mr. Swift's paper was passing through the press. See 2 Massachusetts Historical Society's Proceedings for February, 1895, ix. 410 et seq.

to be added. Some of the sermons have passed to the honor of more than one edition; such cases I have sought to notice in passing.

YEARS IN WHICH NO SERMONS WERE PREACHED.

1635, 1636, 1639, 1640, 1642, 1647, 1650–1655, 1662, 1687, 1688, 1691, 1752, 1764.

SERMONS PREACHED BUT NOT KNOWN TO HAVE BEEN PRINTED.

1634. John Cotton.	1664. Richard Mather.
1637. Thomas Shepard.	1665. John Russell.
1638. Thomas Shepard.	1666. Thomas Cobbett.
1641. Nathaniel Ward.	1669. John Davenport.
1643. Ezekiel Rogers.	1675. Joshua Moody.
1644. Richard Mather.	1678. Samuel Phillips.
1645. John Norton.	1680. Edward Bulkley.
1646. Edward Norris.	1681. William Brimsmead.
1648. Zechariah Symmes.	1684. John Hale.
1649. Thomas Cobbett.	1686. Michael Wigglesworth.
1656. Charles Chauncy.	1692. Joshua Moody.
1657. John Norton.	1697. John Danforth.
1658. Jonathan Mitchel.	1713. Samuel Treat.
1659. John Eliot.	1717. Roland Cotton.
1660. Richard Mather.	1875. Edwin C. Bolles.

Of these, however, Mather in 1644, Cobbett in 1649, Moody in 1675, Hale in 1684, Wigglesworth in 1686, Treat in 1713, Cotton in 1717, and Bolles in 1875 were asked by the Court to furnish a copy for the press. Shepard's for 1638 exists in outline as elsewhere described; Richard Mather's for 1660 was quoted by Mitchel seven years later as if printed; the Magnalia speaks of Davenport's for 1669 as "afterwards published;" while Moody's for 1692 is in Haven's list. These and other of the missing sermons have been touched upon more fully in due order throughout the foregoing pages of this list.